I0740246

THE EXILED OTHERKIN

BOOKS BY D. LIEBER

Minte and Magic

The Exiled Otherkin

The Assassin's Legacy

Intended Fates

Intended Bondmates

Intended Strangers

Intended Enemies

Council of Covens

Dancing with Shades

In Search of a Witch's Soul

Also by D. Lieber

Conjuring Zephyr

Once in a Black Moon

A Very Witchy Yuletide

The Treason of Robyn Hood

The Curse of Moonseed Manor

The Goblin King's Mischief

The Winter Sorcerer and the Summer Witch

Bitten by the North Wind

THE EXILED OTHERKIN

A MINTE AND MAGIC ADVENTURE

D. LIEBER

Ink & Magick, LLC
Kenosha, Wisconsin
contact@inkandmagick.com

Hardcover ISBN: 978-1-951239-05-3
Paperback ISBN: 978-1-7328323-3-6
Ebook ISBN: 978-1-7328323-4-3

Cover art by Black Rose Writing
Title text design by Maria Spada
Edited by Cover to Cover Editing

SPECIAL THANKS

To my husband, John, who challenges me to be the best version of myself.

Thank you to all of my friends, family, and beta readers. I couldn't have done it without your support. Thanks Amy, Megan, Laura, Mary, Debbie, Karissa, Kyla, Paul, T.J., Mike, Alan, Gaylan, Michelle, David, Katerina, Mom, and the Kenosha Steampunk Society.

I entered the unfamiliar group of trees, looking over my shoulder to see if Liam had changed his mind. As I watched the shimmering door close behind me and disappear, I wasn't surprised or upset he'd chosen to stay. Learning from his example, I abandoned all further thought of him and moved forward into the unknown.

This realm looks similar enough.

I approached a clearing and exited the trees.

Or... not.

A collection of large buildings sprawled before me for as far as I could see. I'd never seen so many tall structures. I slowly descended the stone steps that were wedged into the hill on which I stood, drawn forward by wonder. People shouted greetings at each other while they bustled along cobbled roads and in and out of buildings. Horse hooves clopped on the stones as they pulled carriages and carts toward unknown destinations.

A dark mass moved overhead, blackening the

sky. I crouched, covering my head and neck, and prepared for impact. When nothing happened, I peeked up at the flying ship, held aloft by a curious floating bubble. After determining it wasn't in danger of falling on me, I followed the ship from the ground as it traveled above the buildings.

Fascinated, I peered through shop windows. There were all manner of wares: clothes, food, and shiny metal devices that moved by themselves.

Because I kept stopping to look into windows, I had to run to keep the flying ship in sight. It landed in a field, which contained a series of wooden platforms with other ships docked at them. A door opened in the side of the hull, creating a ramp where humans disembarked and began unloading boxes. I studied the flying ship, mesmerized. The bubble seemed to be made of cloth. A table near the dock had a sign that read:

Hiring Crew

Perfect. A moving target is difficult to find. I have no confidence she'll leave me be just because I'm a realm away.

I approached the table, and a burly man looked up from his papers.

"Name?" he asked gruffly.

"Ember."

"Ember..." He trailed off like it wasn't enough.

Of course he doesn't know me by just my first name. Well, I certainly can't give him my clan and branch information.

"Ember Otherkin." I smiled inwardly at my private joke.

"Have you ever worked on a merchant airship before, Ember Otherkin?" He squinted at me skeptically.

"No, but I'm useful to have around," I said with confidence.

He continued to eye me, unsure. "What're your skills?"

"I'm a good fighter, fast and strong."

"We don't have much need for fighters. How're you at climbing?"

"I have good balance and can hold my own weight plus more."

"Great. You can be our new rigger."

He handed me a piece of paper with the details of my contract. I signed it, and he stamped it.

"Report back at dawn," he said, shaking my hand.

I guess I have time to kill before we leave. I had no human money, but I wandered around the nearby shops. *I'll be living here from now on. I need to be able to fit in.*

I looked at my reflection in a shop window. Self-conscious, I checked to make sure my dark hair covered the tips of my pointed ears. *I suppose I'm passably human. If Helena hadn't stripped my magic before banishing me, I could easily cover my ears with a glamour.*

I clenched my fists and teeth, digging my fingernails into my palms to squelch my need to punch something. A scuffling sound came from an alley to the left. Curious, I investigated. Two large men held a young man by the arms while another hit him repeatedly. The slight youth's blond head slumped on his chest. The assailant grabbed his hair and lifted his face up to strike him again. The blood streaming from his nose glistened in the dim light. A cut marred his pale cheek, and one eye looked painfully swollen.

I smiled to myself. *It looks like I'll get to relieve my anger after all.*

They didn't see me coming. I took out the attacker first, sweeping his legs from under him. The other two dropped their prey, and he went down hard. I had expected some satisfaction from the fight, but they didn't provide. After a few well-placed punches and kicks, they fled the alley.

Novices.

I approached the young man and rolled him to his back. I checked his pulse, and it beat hard and strong.

Now what do I do with him?

His eyes fluttered open and focused on me. He sat up quickly. The movement made him unsteady, and his head fell toward the ground. *Whoa!* I caught him before he cracked his skull. Meeting my eyes, he smiled weakly.

"Thank you," he whispered.

He sat up slowly the second time and pulled a handkerchief from his pocket. Trying to wipe the blood from his face, he smeared it across his cheek. I sighed internally as I watched and snatched the rag from him to wipe his face properly.

"Why did they beat you?" I asked as he winced while I cleaned his face.

He shrugged. "When I asked them for food, they told me to give them money. I guess they were angry I didn't have any."

I looked at him more closely. His clothes hung loosely on his slight frame. In between the bruises and scrapes, his skin was pallid. I handed him the handkerchief and removed my pack. My hand found the bread I'd taken before leaving Faerie, and I passed it to him. He devoured it like he hadn't eaten in days.

I stood to leave, and he rose to go with me, wobbling a little at the knees. I turned a cold stare on him that said, "Do not follow me." He didn't seem to notice and shadowed me anyway.

"Well, goodbye," I said at the mouth of the alley.

"Take me with you."

"No."

"Please."

"No."

"I won't be a burden."

"You're already a burden."

"My name is Reilley. What's yours?"

"Go away." I left, but he kept pace with me. *This is why I don't help people.*

Though his face was battered, he smiled cheerfully. "Where are we going?"

"I don't know where *you're* going, but it's not with me."

He continued to pursue me, undeterred.

Finally, I turned on him. "Why're you following me?"

He flinched at my harsh tone, and his smile

faltered. "I want to go with you," he murmured, his green eyes pleading.

Shit. "Look, you can't go with me. I sail with a merchant airship tomorrow."

"You work on an airship? Can I see it?"

He smiled innocently, and I let out an exasperated sigh.

"Fine. But after I show you, will you go your own way?"

He nodded enthusiastically, so I sighed again and motioned for him to follow me.

We marched to the dock, and I pointed to the airship.

"There. You saw it. Now, you can go."

He ignored me and stared at the ship with sparkling eyes. Reilley's gaze found the recruiter still sitting at the table, and he dashed toward him. Seeing his purpose, I rushed after him. He'd reached the burly man before I could catch him.

"Name?"

"Reilley Nai," he panted, trying to catch his breath.

"What're your skills?"

"I'm a great cook."

He took in Reilley's hungry appearance. "What's your experience?"

"I grew up working at my parents' inn. I often helped in the kitchen."

"We do need another cook..." he mumbled. "All right, kid, how old are you?"

"Twenty-two."

We both looked at him with raised eyebrows. *We're that close to the same age? He looks so young.*

"Let me see your papers." The recruiter held out his hand, squinting at him with a hard mouth.

Reilley shuffled his feet. "They burned when the inn caught fire."

"Then I need your parents to sign permission, stating your age."

He looked down and answered quietly. "My parents were lost in the fire, too."

The burly man gave him a heavy nod and turned to me. "Otherkin, take Nai to Records and bring me proof he's twenty-two."

I opened my mouth to protest. *I really need this job.* "Aye, Sir," I ground out.

Reilley bounced with joy as we left the dock.

"Where's Records?" I asked Reilley. *I don't know anything about this place.*

"Near City Hall, but it'll be closing soon."

We hurried through the crowded streets while trying not to bump into too many people. A trail of annoyed protests followed in our wake. One vegetable stall vendor let out a particularly colorful string of curses when Reilley knocked into his cabbages. My heart sped up when I looked over my shoulder and saw he was chasing us. I let out a breathy laugh when he settled for throwing a cabbage after us.

Records turned out to be a small room with a polished wood floor. The walls were off-white and featured portraits of greying men who stared stonily at everyone who entered their domain. We stepped up to a tall, orderly desk, and the neat man sitting behind it looked over his spectacles at us.

"We need proof of age," I told him.

"Name?"

"Reilley Nai."

"Place of birth?"

I looked at Reilley.

"Sutton," he responded.

"Year of birth?"

"1995."

Has that much time passed in the human realm? Time really does flow differently in Faerie.

The man nodded and pulled a tube, which jutted from the wall, toward him. "Proof of age, Sutton, 1995, Nai, Reilley," he pronounced into the tube. "Please step aside." He motioned us to wait.

After a while, a clicking came from the doorway behind the counter. It grew louder, and a cart with wheels attached to two metal bars affixed to the floor appeared. It had a large key on the side that slowly spun as it moved, and it stopped behind the counter. The man in spectacles took a volume from the cart and opened it to a marked page.

"Yes, Nai, Reilley. Born March 5, 1995 in Sutton to Mr. James Nai and Mrs. Mary Nai, née Sheffield. All is in order." He made a note on a piece of paper and stamped it. Then he handed it to Reilley. They locked the door behind us as we left Records.

Returning to the dock, we didn't find the recruiter. We approached the ship and asked the guard where he'd gone.

"Mr. Brewster has retired for the evening."

"He asked us to bring him proof of age," I explained.

"Ember and Reilley?" the guard asked.

We nodded. He knocked on the side of the hull, and the hatch opened. We climbed into the cargo hold. A man on the inside closed the hatch behind us.

"We have something for Mr. Brewster," I told the sandy-haired man who'd closed the hatch.

"New recruits, eh?" He sized us up.

I nodded, squinting at him hard as he eyed me.

"Welcome aboard. I'm Shy." He held out his hand.

"Ember." I shook his hand firmly.

"Hey, Shy. I'm Reilley." Reilley smiled brightly.

I glanced sideways at Reilley's upbeat demeanor. *His cheerfulness is a little irksome.*

We followed Shy through the packed cargo hold. Reaching a steep flight of stairs, we climbed up to the next deck. A long hallway stretched before us with doors on either side.

"This is the quarterdeck. Mr. Brewster is the first mate." He knocked on a door on the right, and Mr. Brewster stuck his head out.

"What is it, Masters?"

"Recruits to see you, Sir." Shy stepped aside so Brewster could see us.

Reilley handed him the paper. The first mate read it and nodded.

"Come in and sign your contract." He opened the door to reveal a cramped but cozy room with no personal possessions in sight. The bed, table, and chair were standard size, but I had a difficult time imagining Brewster fitting into them. A shelf with books and rolled maps looked well organized and frequently used.

Reilley signed the contract, and Brewster stamped it.

As he was about to dismiss us, Reilley asked, "Mr. Brewster, Sir, may I stay on board tonight? I don't have anywhere else to sleep."

Brewster stared stone-faced and grunted. "Fine. Masters, show them to their bunks. Unless you're leaving for the night, Otherkin?"

"No, Sir."

He nodded and shooed us from the room.

"What jobs were you given?" Shy asked as he shut Brewster's door.

"Cook," Reilley said brightly.

"Rigger."

Shy's smile faltered a little, and I narrowed my eyes.

We followed Shy as he walked farther down the hall. Turning left, the room opened into a kitchen and mess hall.

"Reilley, you'll share a bunk with Willie, the other cook." Shy pointed to a door to the left. I thought Reilley would go to his bunk, but he continued to follow us as we walked back to the main hall. At the end, we took stairs to the next deck.

"As you can see, this is engineering."

Men and women dashed around the room, gleaming with sweat and smudged with black smears. The fires burned low. A large furnace at the center of the room had a thick chimney leading from it into the ceiling. Some people were moving piles of what looked like coal while others tended a huge machine. It consisted of a number of large metal coils attached to gears. Some of the coils were wound tight while others were loose. The gears attached to the coils were meshed with gears that had magnets on them. Ropes, made of a material I couldn't identify, were threaded through the center of the magnet gears.

We passed through engineering and climbed to the main deck. The wooden deck sprawled before us. The chimney from engineering came up through the floor and reached toward the cloth bubble above us.

Shy pointed to a cabin on the left. "That's where you'll bunk with the rest of the deckhands, Ember. I still have inventory to do. I trust you both can get settled?" He disappeared below deck.

I walked toward the cabin, and Reilley followed.

"I wish we were bunking together, Ember," he said, slumping his shoulders. I didn't respond and entered the cabin, shutting the door in his face.

2

The small cabin had six cots hung around the room. A well-endowed woman looked up from the book she read. She smiled sincerely at me.

"I'd hoped the new rigger would be a woman. I'm Charlie, the ship's carpenter. I ensure the hull is in good repair."

I shook her outstretched hand. "Ember." My skin prickled in the face of her open smile and friendly tone, but needing information, I smiled back. "Tell me, Charlie. What will I be expected to do as a rigger?"

Her smile faltered. "Mr. Brewster didn't tell you? Maybe you should ask Mac, the boatswain. He can explain it better."

Steeling myself, I leaned toward her and gently bit my lower lip. "Please, Charlie."

She stepped closer to me and lowered her voice. "The rigger is in charge of checking the envelope. You'll be expected to climb on the outside to check the fabric for leaks and tears. If damaged, you have to repair it while we're in the air, if possible." Then she whispered, "Our last rigger fell and died. Captain almost turned down this load because we still don't know if it was an accident."

I let that sink in. *Well, it can't be more dangerous than staying with Helena in Faerie.*

"Are you going to stay?" she asked seriously.

"Why shouldn't I?"

She looked like that should be obvious. "What if it wasn't an accident and someone tries to hurt you?"

"He wouldn't want to do that. I'd have to retaliate," I said darkly.

At the sound of my confidence, she let out a shaky laugh and relaxed into a soft smile. "I have something you might like." She went to her cot and pulled out a bag from behind it. Riffling through, she returned with a brown hat with a short, soft brim and a floppy top. "It may help cover those ears of yours, Princess."

I stared at her hard. Her face shimmered and revealed its true form. Her ears were pointed, like mine, but her eyes were clearly Fae. My human mother's blood softened most of my Fae features, but she looked untamed.

"So the rumors are true. Queen Helena stripped your magic and banished you to the human realm. You can't even see through a glamour."

My heart hammered as she stood between me and the only door. I crouched into a fighting stance.

"Relax. I'm not going to hurt you. I have no loyalty to Queen Helena. Why do you think I'm here? I fled Faerie during the human sympathizer persecutions."

I eased my bunched muscles but stayed guarded.

"It seems we think alike. Stay on the move, and they won't find me, right?"

I nodded.

"There are a lot more of us here than you know."

That made me even more uneasy.

Her expression softened. "I can help you, Princess, if you'll let me."

"Don't call me that."

"Your late father was a good and kind king. I'm sure he'd have stopped the persecutions had he known about them. I pledge my friendship to you in his memory and in the hope you'll live up to his bloodline."

Grief washed over me at the mention of my father. "I don't want to be queen," I ground out.

"You don't have to be, but you have my loyalty either way." She bowed her head to me and waited.

I hesitated. *Many have pledged loyalty to me before, but few were sincere. She could be genuine or false. I'm at a disadvantage right now, and she knows this realm. It'll be easier to keep an eye on her if I play friends.*

Instead of placing my hand on her head in acknowledgment of her loyalty, I bowed my head and touched our foreheads. She looked up with wide eyes.

"If you give me loyalty and friendship, it will be as an equal."

Her untamed eyes swam with tears. "Princess..."

"Ember," I said firmly.

"Ember," she agreed. She replaced her glamour and tugged the hat onto my head and over the tips of my ears. "Perfect." She smiled and motioned to the cot next to hers. We sat in companionable silence for a while.

"So you fled Faerie because you're a human sympathizer?" *I've heard rumors about persecutions, but Papa never found proof.*

She nodded, and her eyes lost focus. "I loved a human once. My parents found out and disowned me."

"What happened to him?"

"My brother killed him," she said, hollow.

I didn't respond.

"Speaking of brothers, yours was just crowned. Though being so young, it's expected that Queen Helena will remain in power until he comes of age." She changed the subject.

Poor Pika. I'm sorry I had to leave you behind, alone, with your mother. I didn't even get to say a proper goodbye.

"Don't worry. There's so much in the human realm. You'll soon forget your old life. Wait until you meet everyone. You'll love it here. Would you like to try some chocolate?"

I shrugged and held out my hand. Popping the brown lump she gave me into my mouth, sweet, creamy bliss invaded my tongue. I'd never tasted anything like it.

"Chocolate?" I asked in wonder.

She smiled knowingly and nodded. "Chocolate."

The door to the cabin opened, and four men entered. All of their eyes focused on me.

"You're back," Charlie said. "This is Ember, our new rigger."

The leader stepped forward. He was a solid man with fire-red hair and deep-sea eyes. "Welcome aboard, Ember. I'm Mac, the boatswain. This is Nick, Indulal, and Sasha."

A mischievous grin spread across Nick's olive face. His curly, black hair flopped as he tilted his head to one side. Indulal dipped his dark head at me serenely.

Sasha came toward me and took my hand. His light eyes sparkled as he placed a kiss on my inner wrist. Gripping his hand, I spun his back to me and held my dagger to his throat.

"Don't ever do that again."

His shocked expression turned to one of enjoyment. "Da, Ember," he purred with a thick accent.

I pushed him away and returned my dagger to its sheath in my boot. Mac, Nick, and Indulal seemed unconcerned by my exchange with Sasha.

"All right, everyone, we start early tomorrow. Hit the sack," Mac said. We all settled into our bunks, and Charlie blew out the lamp. Surrounded by people in the dark cabin, my muscles tightened like there was no room to move. I took a few slow, deep breaths and pictured the open night sky.

No stars shone in the cloudy sky as I wandered around the palace, unable to sleep. Grief from my father's death and tension over what would happen to me next kept me awake a lot recently.

I found myself near Helena's chambers without making the decision to walk that way. I turned quickly to go anywhere else. Then I heard the deep timbre of the voice that whispered in my dreams.

"You wanted to see me, my queen?" Liam asked formally.

"Yes, Liam," Helena said simply. "I have an important assignment for you."

Liam waited for her to continue.

"Are you loyal to me, Liam?"

"Of course, my queen."

"I can't help but feel you only serve me to protect that half-human wretch."

"Of course not, my queen."

"Are you sure? You only started to serve me when I threatened her. Now, how do you think that makes me feel?"

"I am loyal to only you, my queen."

"Yes, I suppose you are. After all, it isn't as if she remained true to you, is it? How many lovers do you think she's had now? It's almost as though I did you a favor. Otherwise, you might have pledged yourself to her and discovered her infidelity when it was too late. How sad, and yet you still haven't given yourself to anyone. Have you, Liam?" Helena stabbed with a sweet tone.

"As you say," Liam responded in a strangled voice.

She seemed pleased to have made an impact. "Exactly right, so you won't mind accepting a very special assignment, will you?"

"Whatever you wish, my queen, it will be done."

"Excellent. This will be for your own good as

well. As you know, Pika is the rightful heir. Unfortunately, there will no doubt be filthy human-lovers who want the wretch on the throne. Therefore, for the stability of Faerie, I'm exiling her to the human realm. Perhaps banished without magic, she cannot interfere any longer."

"What do you wish of me, my queen?"

"Prove your loyalty with this final test: escort her to the portal and ensure she goes through."

Liam paused, and I listened harder to hear his answer. "As you wish, my queen."

I could hear the smile in Helena's response. "What a good and obedient boy you have grown into, Liam. I will certainly reward your loyalty."

"Serving you is reward enough, my queen."

Her voice changed to one thick with heat. "Serving me gives you pleasure, does it? Just how obedient are you, I wonder? Shall we test that as well?"

Liam didn't respond.

"To the bed," Helena commanded in a hard voice.

Silence answered her.

"No response?" she demanded.

"As you wish, my queen," Liam's voice was dead and hollow.

"Good boy," she praised.

I had long let go of Liam. My insides were frozen and immovable; Pika was the only one alive who could reach my heart. I didn't feel sad or angry by what I'd overheard. If anything, it felt inevitable as if everything that had ever happened led up to this moment. However, when I thought about whom I had once been, I knew my past self broke. She shook with wailing sobs, and she still loved him.

As I stood in the dark, I felt nothing. Still, I promised my past self I would give Liam one more chance to save himself. *In honor of what we used to have, I will do this for him.*

I walked toward my room, thinking of what needed to be done. I stopped by the kitchens to grab some bread. The only warm spot left inside me throbbed with sadness. Veering toward Pika's room, I opened the door quietly. Then I crept in and looked down at the sleeping youth.

He'd been affected by Papa's death even more than I, and I worried about how my absence would impact him. Then I fortified myself. *He'll be all right. He's clever and kind. He'll survive and make a great king.*

I returned to my room and hastily packed a small bag with resignation.

The tension of uncertainty had left me, and I finally fell into an exhausted sleep.

I slept until early afternoon when a knock at my door woke me. Even though I should've been rested from sleeping for so long, I felt dull as I walked to the door. Everything seemed dim, like all the colors and sounds had been muted. A haze fogged my perception. I tried to clear it, but it clung to me like a head cold.

I opened the door to find Liam. His eyes, usually hard and cold, seemed broken and a little wild. But as he stared at me, his expression shifted to the stern look that had long ago become the norm.

"Queen Helena has decreed that you be stripped

of your Fae magic and exiled to the human realm. I'm here to escort you to the door."

"When will she strip my magic?" *Maybe I can protect myself from that at least.*

"I've been told it was done while you were asleep. Follow me."

How? I stopped myself from dwelling on how she'd stripped my magic without me knowing. It was useless to understand how when there was nothing I could do.

I grabbed my bag, which he frowned at, and followed him.

Many people stopped what they were doing to watch us pass. I kept my eyes straight ahead and my face unreadable.

Outside the palace gates, it didn't take long before we reached one of the many doors to the human realm.

Liam summoned the portal and stood by to make sure I went through.

I turned to him. "Come with me."

His mouth fell open at my request. He'd made himself clear ten years ago. I had long let go of those feelings and had never spoken of that night. But I'd promised my past self I would try to save him.

The flicker of surprise passed quickly, and his face returned to its stony default.

"No."

My past self reached out desperately, taking control of my mouth. "Liam, please," she begged.

His stony expression slipped a little.

"Goodbye, Ember."

You fool, I chided my past self. *When will you*

learn? My present self back in control, I stepped through the portal.

The comforting ice inside me allowed me to recognize how idiotic my past self was. I welcomed its familiar chill, pushed her back to where she belonged, and went to sleep in the dark cabin.

3

Charlie shook me awake the next morning. I followed the rest of the main deck crew to the quarterdeck for breakfast. Reilley and a short, gruff man, who I assumed was Willie, were setting plates of food on a counter above the stove. Along with my fellow crewmen, I grabbed a plate, then sat at one of the long benches. It seemed we ate in shifts because only some of the engineering crew were present.

The food was palatable but not as good as the food in Faerie, or chocolate. The entire time I ate, Reilley tried to get my attention. I studiously ignored him. Finally, his efforts looked almost painful. I sighed, made eye contact, and nodded to him. He lit up, so pleased that I hadn't forgotten him.

We ate quickly and returned to the main deck. While Nick, Indulal, Sasha, and Charlie went about their regular duties, Mac beckoned me to him.

"Do you understand your duties?"

"Check the fabric. Fix the leaks."

"Right. Let's get your equipment."

I followed him to a shed across from the deckhand cabin. Inside was a variety of neatly organized equipment. He showed me a belt with pockets and straps attached, a cylinder of metal, and spectacles that hugged the face and were fastened by a strap around the back of the head.

"This is your harness and tool belt." He showed me how to step into the leg loops and tighten the belt strap until it fit snugly. He pointed to the edge of the deck where a ladder of rope connected the deck to the envelope.

"On the lowest ladder rung you'll find a carabiner. Clip it to your harness. It's attached to a retractable reel on the top of the envelope. If you tug it quickly twice, it'll reel you to the top. If you pull hard once, it'll loosen the rope, allowing you to rappel."

He shoved the metal cylinder into one of the pockets at the back of my tool belt. "This is your patch spray. If you find a small leak, spray this on it. It plugs the leak and solidifies in seconds. In the belt, there are colored flags, and each one is attached to a carabiner. As you climb around the envelope, you'll come across the ropes that hold the fabric in place. If a section you just checked has no leaks, attach a green flag to the rope and send it down. If there was a small leak and you patched it, send down a yellow flag. If there is a leak that's too big to patch and we need to land, blow this whistle."

He pulled a tin whistle from his pocket and handed it to me. "Those rope ladders are emergency access ladders. If the reel isn't working properly, blow the whistle and one of the deckhands will fetch someone from engineering to climb up and fix the mechanism."

Handing me the spectacles, he said, "Wear your goggles. It can get pretty windy up there. You'll be glad to see. If there's some emergency reason we need you to come down before you're finished, we'll ring the bell repeatedly, meaning all hands on deck. We ring the bell twice for mealtimes. Come down to eat, and resume your duties after. Any questions?"

I shook my head.

"Great. Good luck." He smiled genuinely and went about his own duties.

I shoved the whistle into a free pocket of my tool belt, removed my hat, and put on my goggles. Then I replaced the hat firmly over my ears. Heading toward the ladder, I was reaching for the carabiner when I heard Reilley calling my name.

"Ember, wait!" He heaved deep breaths as if he'd run all the way from the kitchen. I turned to him and waited to see what he wanted. He held out a cloth napkin tied into a bundle.

"In case you get hungry up there, I made you biscuits." He smiled brightly as he placed the napkin-wrapped biscuits in my hand.

"Thank you," I said, shocked by the small kindness.

If possible, his face lit up more. I carefully put the gift in an empty pocket of my belt.

"Be careful," he begged as I attached the carabiner to my harness.

I nodded. "See you at lunch."

I tugged on the rope twice, and the reel lifted me in a controlled ascent. Reilley watched me climb toward the envelope. I concentrated on what I was doing rather than him smiling and waving up at me.

The envelope was a metal frame with fabric stretched over it. At the edge of the fabric, ropes ran through wide grommets, attaching the fabric to the ship. The square pattern of the frame made it easy to walk up the envelope as the reel pulled me.

When I reached the summit, the reel stopped drawing me in, allowing me slack to wander around the top. I started by checking the fabric near the reel. I didn't see any holes, but I ran my hand over the fabric to feel if any air escaped. The metal was warm through the fabric, but it didn't burn me. *The fabric must have heat-resistant qualities.*

Checking every square inch of fabric was tedious work. The wind whipped my face, and I was glad for my hat and goggles.

I followed a systematic pattern for efficiency. Once I'd checked the top, I chose a vertical section, and rappelled down to the base ropes, checking the fabric as I went. Reaching the edge, I ascended to the top and checked the next section as I rappelled. I placed green flags on the first few base ropes as I found no leaks. When I came across my first leak, it was minor. I pulled out the patch spray and popped the cap with my thumb. It hung at the side of the cylinder, attached to the edge. The top of the cylinder had a small white tab with a little circle on one side.

That must be where the spray comes out.

I pointed the circle toward the leak and pressed my finger to the tab. Foul smelling liquid shot from the hole and coated the leak and surrounding fabric.

Seconds later, hot air no longer escaped the envelope, and the area where I had sprayed was firm but pliable. I sent a yellow flag down the next base rope.

My stomach grumbled. The next time I reached the top, I took a break. I pulled out Reilley's gift and carefully unwrapped the biscuits. A little crumbled but still edible, they had a creamy golden color. I broke off a small piece and chewed it tentatively. It was soft and buttery with a flakey texture. I closed my eyes and savored the taste. They were gone too quickly.

He really is a good cook.

Reenergized, I resumed my work. I found a few more small leaks. When I was about a third of the way finished with the envelope, I heard two rings of the bell.

Mealtime.

I rappelled down, still checking as I went, and sent down a green flag. Then I descended the nearest ladder to the main deck and clipped my carabiner on the lowest rung.

I met Charlie as I put my equipment away.

"How's it coming?" she asked.

"Fine."

She examined the clouds above us. "It's a nice day for it. It's rough when the weather is bad. How far did you get?"

I nodded to the flags at the bases of the ropes. "About a third of the way."

"Not bad, and you'll get faster as you get used to it."

We descended to the mess hall. I acknowledged Reilley as I grabbed a plate and then sat in between

Charlie and Mac. Sasha flashed a smile at me and Charlie from across the table.

"Charlie. Ember," he purred.

"Sasha." I gave him a no-nonsense look.

"Don't get too upset. You get used to it," Charlie whispered to me. "He's harmless, really. He won't do anything without your consent."

If that's true, I guess I can relent a little.

"All right, guys, eat quickly. We'll be landing soon. Ember, when you see us descending to land, climb down immediately. It's too dangerous to be up there while we're landing," Mac instructed. I nodded my acknowledgment, and we all ate hurriedly and returned to work.

I was halfway finished checking the envelope when we began our descent. I rappelled down to the main deck as Mac had ordered. Charlie was collecting materials when I met her on the main deck.

"Our jobs only get more demanding once we land. Repairs are easier when we're at a standstill. The other deckhands will go to the cargo hold to unload boxes and load the next shipment. Then they get liberty until we're ready to leave. If we're lucky, you and I will get finished in time to have a little fun before we sail again," Charlie said.

The descent didn't take long. Once we'd landed, I scrambled to finish checking the envelope. Charlie had been right. I checked the rest of the fabric in almost half the time. There were fewer people in the mess hall at dinner; most had gone ashore to eat.

Reilley caught my attention as I grabbed a plate. "Ember, are you going ashore after you eat?"

I shrugged. "Probably."

"Can I go with you? I have to buy ingredients."

"Why don't you just go with Willie?"

Reilley winced.

"Because that's the boy's job. I have things to do too, you know," Willie spat.

I didn't acknowledge Willie's abrasive tone. "When will you be ready?" I asked Reilley.

"Everyone else has eaten. Once you all are finished, I can go," he said excitedly.

I nodded. "Meet me on the dock."

I sat between Mac and Charlie. Sasha, Indulal, and Nick weren't there.

"How much do you have left?" Mac asked me.

"I'm finished. There were no major leaks. What should I do now?"

Mac seemed impressed I'd completed the checks already. "Leave the flags. I want to see which sections needed repairs. I'll put them away. Good work." He smiled.

Charlie had almost completed her repairs. She said she'd show us around, so I promised to meet her on the dock.

After I'd finished eating, I grabbed my pack from my bunk and descended a ladder from the main deck to the dock. Mr. Brewster stood beside a woman with a demanding presence. Her blonde hair was cut short, and she was all business as she talked with another man about shipments.

Seeing me land on the dock, Brewster walked toward me. "Good work, Otherkin," he praised, handing me a clinking pouch. "As promised, you'll be paid at every port."

I put the pouch in my jacket pocket.

"Thank you, Sir."

Brewster followed my gaze to the imposing woman and answered my unspoken question. "That would be our captain," he said proudly.

I nodded my understanding.

"Ember!" Reilley cried excitedly as he slid down the ladder.

I just looked at him.

Brewster gave Reilley his pay and returned to the captain.

"Come on!" Reilley started to run from the dock.

I grabbed the back of his shirt. "We have to wait for Charlie," I said as he looked over his shoulder at me.

"That woman with the hammer? I like her. She's nice," he gushed.

Charlie's heavy boots thumped on the dock. "Thanks for waiting," she said and collected her pay from Brewster.

Reilley told her what he needed for the kitchen, and we left the dock. Reilley and I took in our surroundings. His head swiveled rapidly with delight, but I swept my eyes slowly and deliberately. Like the city we'd left that morning, there was a large collection of buildings. However, these buildings were shorter and more picturesque. There were still crowded streets and carriages, but the smells from the food shops were better. This city just felt different, more carefree.

Charlie led us down a few streets, knowing exactly where she was going. She let us stop along the way and look in the shop windows. She was much more tolerant of Reilley's energy than I. She smiled at him fondly whenever he burst with enthusiasm. Eventually, she directed us into a shop that sold herbs and spices.

Reilley pulled out a list and talked to the shopkeeper. Charlie and I browsed as he purchased what he needed. A blue bottle on a shelf caught my eye. I pulled the cork and placed the opened bottle under my nose. A familiar pungent odor wafted from the bottle. *Witch hazel.* I'd used it many times and knew exactly what it was good for.

Charlie approached the clerk with me to purchase the tincture. The wispy old man nearly dropped the coin I placed in his hand. I looked at him, curious. His wide eyes met mine, and he hastily bowed. Alarmed, I turned to Charlie.

"Philippe runs a safehouse for refugees," Charlie whispered.

I looked back at Philippe. His face shimmered for just a second and revealed untamed eyes and a much younger face with dark hair. Another blink and the wispy old man stood before me.

"We truly support your claim, Princess. Surely *you* understand our attachment to humans," he said softly and bowed again.

"Please, don't draw attention. I don't want a claim. Let me live a new life here," I pleaded. My eyes located Reilley across the shop to ensure he was out of hearing range.

"But Princess, you're the elder child. You're the rightful heir."

"Stop calling me that!"

Reilley looked up at my outburst, and Charlie placed a soothing hand on my shoulder.

"She wants to live peacefully among her mother's people, Philippe," Charlie explained.

He winced but bowed. "As you wish. But please know there are those who support you and would help you."

My heart welled, and I beat it down. "Thank you," I said shortly. I grabbed my purchase and quickly left the shop. By the time Charlie and Reilley joined me outside, my head was on straight again.

4

Charlie led us to the other shops Reilley needed to visit: a butcher shop, a bakery, and a fruit and vegetable stand. Since we couldn't possibly carry all that Reilley purchased, he directed the shop owners deliver the food to the ship.

Taking a break, we sat on the edge of a fountain at the center of a plaza. I sat sideways with one leg dangling on the outside of the fountain while my elbow rested on my other knee. The light from the streetlamps shimmered on the rippling surface of the water and lit up the spray like fireflies.

My eyes lost focus, and my mind drifted.

I chased fireflies in the garden just after dusk. Lughnasadh was the next day, so everyone in our village was preparing for the celebration. The air was warm and carried the scent of the blackberry tarts my mother was baking. We'd picked the berries that very morning. The smell made my mouth water, and I abandoned my firefly hunt to rush home.

Maybe Mama will let me have one early.

The door to our cottage was open, and light from the fireplace flickered into the night. I crept toward the doorway.

A large hand covered my mouth as an arm wrapped around my stomach. Wide-eyed and prepared to scream, I looked up at my snatcher. My father's reassuring face looked down at me. He removed his hand, and I took a deep breath to squeal my welcome. He placed a finger to my lips, telling me to be quiet.

"I missed you, little cub," he whispered as he nuzzled me. The warm glow of his presence filled me. He returned me to the ground and looked at me seriously. "Little cub, I want you to stay here. Can you do that for me?"

I nodded and watched him sneak toward the open door. Peeking around the doorframe, he gasped and hurried inside. "No, no, no!" he cried. I ran toward him to comfort him but stopped in the doorway. My chest tightened when I saw my father kneeling on the ground sobbing. His back was to me, and he cradled my mother's torso. A dark liquid seeped into the dirt floor around where he sat.

"Papa...?" I took a step forward.

"Ember." His voice cracked. "Please listen to me. I want you to close your eyes."

I closed my eyes tightly, and he placed a soft cloth over them and tied it around the back of my head.

"Little cub, can you sit quietly by the fire while I take care of your mama?"

"What's wrong with her? Will she be all right?"

"I'll explain everything later. Right now, I need to take care of her quickly. Then we're going on a journey."

"But Papa, Lughnasadh is tomorrow. Will we miss the festival?"

"I'm afraid so, little cub, but it will be a great adventure."

Excited about the prospect of going with him, I sat quietly by the fire and didn't remove the cloth from my eyes. I heard him go outside and move around in the garden. After a while, he returned, and I heard the pouring and splashing of water in the washbasin. He shuffled some things around near my bed and returned to me.

"Okay, little cub. Are you ready to go on that adventure?"

"But what about Mama?"

"I'll explain on the way." He lifted me into his arms and carried me outside. "Ignite." The night went silent as if the only sound that existed was his demand.

"Where are we going, Papa?"

"Some place where I can protect you, little cub."

I rested my chin on his shoulder and wrapped my arms around his neck. Through the cloth over my eyes, I could see a bright light in the direction of our cottage.

"Ember?"

My eyes refocused on the light rippling in the fountain. I lifted my head and looked into Reilley's bruised face.

"Charlie said she'd be right back," he said quietly.

I nodded, trying to shake off the fog of memory.

Reilley's worried expression reminded me of the tincture I'd purchased. I reached into my pack and pulled out the blue bottle and a handkerchief. After removing the cork, I dripped the liquid onto the cloth. Reilley leaned in, curious about what I was doing. I raised the handkerchief and placed it gently to Reilley's bruised eye. He looked at me tenderly.

"This is witch hazel. It'll help your bruises heal faster," I explained softly and continued to hold the handkerchief to his face. After a few minutes, I removed it and handed him the recorked bottle.

"Apply it a few times a day," I directed.

"Thank you, Ember." He smiled at me. Appreciation and admiration gleamed in his eyes.

I broke eye contact and nodded. Clearing my throat, I ignored the heat in my face as I scanned the plaza for a distraction.

A shop across the way had some of those metal devices that moved by themselves in the window. I crossed the plaza and looked at them through the glass.

"They're pretty, aren't they? My mother had one like that," Reilley said, pointing at a copper box with silver leaves etched into it.

"What is it?" I whispered to myself.

"It's a music box," he explained without judgment. "Do you want to see it?"

Yes. "No, we should wait for Charlie."

"It's all right. She'll find us." He grabbed my hand and pulled me into the shop. I didn't resist but let go as soon as we were inside. After grabbing the music box from the window, Reilley turned it over to reveal a key stuck in the bottom. He twisted the key a few times and handed it to me. Clear tinkling notes emanated from the box as the key spun by itself.

"Oh, I know this song." Reilley hummed with the tune.

I stared at the box, amazed by its magic. *Humans have things like this?*

When the song stopped, Reilley turned to me. "Do you know the song, Ember?"

I shook my head. "No, but it's lovely."

"It's called *Titania*. It has words too. It's about the queen of the faeries. Do you want to hear the words?"

"No," I said flatly and put the box down.

"But you said you liked it..."

I left the shop, and he followed. Charlie waited for us at the fountain. She smiled and held out a bundle to me. I took it with raised eyebrows. The scent of lavender and roses wafted from the bundle.

"I went back to Philippe's shop to get you a welcome gift. It's soap and shampoo."

I'd only remembered to pack clothes and food. Touched by her kindness, I nodded to her. "Thank you," I murmured.

"Glad I could help." She smiled at me.

She pulled a round disc from her pocket and

looked at it. It had numbers near the edge of the circle and three sticks that pointed at the numbers. One of the sticks moved around the circle quickly.

"It's time we got back to the ship. We sail early again tomorrow," she said and returned the disc to her pocket.

We followed her back to the dock and boarded the ship.

Reilley didn't seem happy about returning to his bunk. When Charlie and I walked toward the deckhand cabin, he didn't go to the quarterdeck. Rather, he wandered around the main deck aimlessly.

"Reilley, you should go get some rest," Charlie encouraged.

He nodded and meandered toward the stairs. I didn't see him go down because Charlie ushered me into our cabin.

"I bet you're ready to wash up. I know I am," she said, grabbing her bath things from near her cot.

I unwrapped the bundle she'd given me in the plaza. A bar of rose-scented soap lay creamy and pink next to a bottle of purple-tinted liquid. I uncorked the bottle, and the scent of lavender made me breathe deep and exhale with satisfaction.

"Ready?" Charlie prompted.

I shoved my soap and shampoo into my pack and grabbed the lot. We exited the cabin and entered a neighboring door. The small room contained a toilet, a sink, a cabinet, and what looked like two closets with glass doors. Charlie opened one of the doors and motioned toward two handles at waist level.

"This is a shower. Turn the left knob for hot water and right for cold. The water comes out there."

I stared up at the spout she pointed to in wonder.

"Wait here. I'll go to the laundry room and fetch some towels."

I pulled the soap and shampoo from my pack and placed them on the cabinet. Then I removed a change of clothes. I hadn't brought many with me, but I had enough for a few days until I could wash the dirty ones. I removed my boots and over-shirt and waited for Charlie in my pants and undershirt.

A sound at the door alerted me that Charlie's hands were too full to open it. I turned the knob and opened it for her.

Charlie wasn't there, no one was.

"Charlie?" I stepped outside and looked around.

An unfamiliar clicking sounded nearby. Click... click...click...

I looked around but couldn't determine its origin. Click...click... It grew closer.

Something brushed the back of my neck. I felt it latch onto my hair and crawl onto my shoulder, clicking as it moved.

Swallowing a scream, I grabbed the unknown and yanked it toward the ground in front of me.

A yelp from above preceded a loud "oof" as Nick landed on his face.

His body shook with silent laughter. A metal spider with legs that clicked as they twitched lay next to him. A string ran from the spider to his hand. His laughter burst from him as he rolled to his back and clutched his stomach. Tears streamed down his face.

The jolt of anger that followed my initial fright dissipated with his infectious sounds of amusement.

My lips stretched into an unfamiliar smile, and I unwittingly started to giggle. After a while, Nick took a few deep breaths and stood.

"I should've known you'd get the upper hand in the end after what you did to Sasha, but I had to try," he said, bending to pick up his spider.

Charlie ascended the stairs with her arms full of fluffy, white towels. She paused to take in the scene.

"Was Nick subjecting you to his welcome of scaring the pants off people? The spider, huh? That one made me scream so loud I nearly broke glass."

Nick smiled innocently. My smile slipped into the polite mask I was used to wearing.

"Next time, I'll win," Nick whispered to me.

I shot back a challenge with my eyes. He walked away pleased, and I opened the washroom door for Charlie.

We stripped down and showered. It was so nice to feel clean. I thanked Charlie for the soap and shampoo again and left to stow my pack next to my cot.

Not wanting to lie down with wet hair, I decided to walk the main deck until it dried. Hat in hand, I strolled leisurely, enjoying the breeze. Halfway down the deck, the thick chimney made the air around it warm and comfortable. I walked around its base and found a rolled up sack. Upon closer inspection, I realized the sack was Reilley wrapped in a blanket. He slept soundly, curled into a ball. His blond head tilted uncomfortably to one side.

Why are you out here? You've had a hard life, haven't you? What've you been doing since your parents died?

He wiggled and snuffled in his sleep. I removed my jacket and balled it up. Approaching carefully, I gently lifted his soft, blond head and placed my jacket under it.

He looks much more comfortable now. I nodded to myself with satisfaction. The warm glow I felt was strange and unfamiliar. I shook myself. *I don't want to hear him complain about a stiff neck later.*

The comforting cold smothered the warmth, and I felt calmer. Its chill was brisk and refreshing. I brushed the hair from my eyes. It was dry.

Slamming my hat back on, I quickly returned to the cabin and my cot. The light was already out. I lay in the dark, trying too hard to fall asleep.

How can Reilley sleep so easily?

His sweet expression as he slept drifted on the backs of my eyelids. Picturing his slow, even breathing had me slipping into sleep.

The memory of my father's agony over my mother's murder must've freed a few other memories because my dreams were a series of scenes long filed away in the hope I'd never see them again.

I hated that the palace was so big and my room was so far away from my father's. As was common practice when I felt lonely, I went to visit him in his study.

The candle on his desk illuminated his creased brow as he perused papers.

"What's wrong, Papa?" I asked, making my way into his room to stand by his chair.

He looked down at me and smiled lovingly. "How are you, little cub? Did you have fun with Liam again today?"

I grinned. "I did. We had a race, and I won."

"Of course, you did. It's because you're the best."

I glowed with his praise, and he patted my head with affection.

"What are you working on?" I asked, climbing onto his lap.

"There seems to be trouble with some of the other clans."

"Are they sick?"

"It doesn't appear that way. It seems many Fae are leaving Faerie and going to the human realm."

"Is that bad?"

"Not in and of itself, but I can't figure out why they're leaving and why so many are leaving at once."

"Maybe they fell in love with humans like you did with Mama."

He smiled at her memory and laughed at my deduction. "Maybe. Wouldn't it be wonderful if that's all it was?"

"Do you think I'll fall in love with a human, too?"

"I don't know, little cub. But don't you like the boys in Faerie?"

"I like Liam."

"Is that so?" He smiled down at me. "And do you love Liam, little cub?"

I made a face that made him chuckle. "Not like that."

"Perhaps you aren't ready for love yet," he countered hopefully.

"I am!" I protested.

"All right, but what if you have a hard time choosing? You're a princess now, and there'll be many boys who want to marry you when the time comes. How will you choose?"

"Like with Stepmother?"

His face darkened a little, but he nodded. "Just like that."

"How did you choose, Papa?"

"Well, I had help from advisors. Helena is from the Air Clan, who held the throne not long ago. She probably would've married your uncle if he hadn't loved your aunt so dearly."

"Will I have to marry someone from the Air Clan too?"

"You can marry whoever you want, little cub. But, should the time come and you have no preference, we'll find someone who will be good for you and Faerie."

"What clan will he be from?" I wondered.

"Well, what clan comes next in the cycle?" he asked.

I scrunched up my face in thought. "Earth?"

He shook his head. "Haven't you been paying attention to your lessons?" he playfully chided me.

"Water! Water comes after Fire," I exclaimed.

He smiled. "Very good. Now, you pay attention to Master Eamonn's lessons. You could be Queen one day. What he's teaching you is very important."

"I don't want to be Queen," I protested.

"Well, you're the only heir right now," he sympathized.

"But I will have a baby brother or sister soon, won't I?"

His eyes grew sad, the way they did when he thought about Mama...

...I gripped the branch I sat on tightly as Liam climbed into the tree next to me. He smiled mischievously, then whispered, "Shh, I think Master Eamonn is coming"

I clamped my lips closed, trying not to laugh so as not to give away our position.

It wasn't Master Eamonn who stepped into the garden, but Helena and her cousin, who was visiting. They looked so graceful with their flowing gowns and long, dark hair.

"So have you made any progress?" Helena's cousin asked her as they strolled.

"None," Helena sighed.

"But you've been married for years," her cousin gasped.

"Don't think I haven't tried," Helena sneered. "He isn't interested. He won't even touch me. That human of his is still firmly lodged in his heart, and I fear her offspring is a constant reminder of her."

"Well, what are you going to do? Do we need to take care of her?" she whispered.

"Not as of yet. I can be patient for a little longer."

Her cousin wasn't placated. "Faerie needs another heir. What will the Fae do if you can't produce one? Put the halfling on the throne?"

"Bite your tongue," Helena snapped. "It will not come to that. I will have my way. Besides, with the exile of the human-lovers, no one will be left to support her claim."...

..."Can't I come with you, Papa?"

"I'm sorry, little cub. Not this time. It'll be far too dangerous."

"But I'm a good fighter," I protested.

"I know you are. That's why I need you to stay here and protect Helena and Pika for me. Can you do that?"

I looked over my shoulder and stared at my baby brother in his mother's arms. "I will protect them, Papa. Don't worry."

"I knew I could count on you, little cub." He smiled at me and kissed my forehead. Then he kissed Pika and whispered to Helena, "Take care of them for me."

"Of course, my dear," she promised.

I tried not to cry as Papa rode out of the palace gates. When I turned back to Helena and Pika, all of Helena's loving concern had vanished.

"I wonder what would happen if the king wasn't here to protect you."

Fear thundered through my veins as it always did when I was left alone with Helena and she wore that pleasant smile.

5

A jolt of panic woke me from my sleep. The calm of predawn hung in the deckhand cabin. The others were still sleeping, so I crept quietly out the door and went to wash my face. I gratefully embraced my inner ice as it pushed the residual memories back into the past where they belonged.

Reilley hummed cheerfully at the stove when I went down for breakfast. Willie was his unpleasant self. I acknowledged Reilley's smile and wave with a stone-faced nod. My lack of expression didn't dampen his mood. Sitting with the rest of the deckhands, Mac was already giving everyone instructions.

"Since we'll be flying for days without docking, you guys will start sleeping in shifts. Charlie and Ember, you'll still sleep at night and work when it's daylight. Try to get all of your work completed before sunset. Your jobs are more dangerous after dark. Indulal, you and I will take the morning shift.

Sasha and Nick, you take tonight. Rest up so you aren't tired."

We finished eating and went about our duties. Grabbing my equipment, I prepared to head up the envelope. Reilley caught me again. He gave me more biscuits and returned my jacket.

"Thank you for lending it to me. It definitely helped me sleep."

"Why weren't you sleeping in your bunk?"

"I just like it out here."

Not buying it, I stared at him without blinking. His face colored.

"Well, I didn't want to bother Willie."

"How were you bothering him?"

"I just think he prefers to be alone. I hear him muttering to himself about how much better the previous cook was. He didn't talk so much or make so much noise. I felt bad for being a nuisance, so I slept up here. I was out of the way, and I didn't bother anyone."

Anger churned in my cold stomach, and I stifled a sneer. I clenched my fists and stomped toward the kitchen to give Willie a piece of my mind. I was aware of a fluttering around me and ignored it until Reilley stopped me in my tracks. He held me in place with his hands on my shoulders. He was surprisingly strong for someone so slight.

"Ember, wait. It really isn't a big deal. I was perfectly comfortable last night. I hate being a bother to others."

His desperate voice and bent head stopped me much more effectively than his hands on my shoulders.

Why should I get in a fight for him anyway?

I broke our contact and attached the carabiner to ascend the envelope. My anger didn't wane as I concentrated on my work. It burned in the back of my mind.

Why does Willie get to make Reilley upset? Hasn't he had enough to deal with in his life? Why do I care what Willie is doing or how Reilley feels? I don't.

The weather was fair again. Because of my repairs the day before, I found no leaks by the time the meal bell rang.

My anger at Willie had simmered to irritation, mostly at myself for even caring. Reilley was not in the kitchen when I went to the mess hall for lunch. I narrowed my eyes at Willie suspiciously.

"Where's Reilley?" I accused.

He sighed at me irritably. "The boy is on night shift if it's any of your business."

My mind raged as I went to the table. I stabbed at my food and ate with jerking motions.

"Are you bothered?" Indulal asked me.

"No."

My retort didn't rock his calm boat. He just nodded in response. I ate and returned to work. I found no tears as I continued to check the envelope. I didn't finish before the meal bell rang again, but I did finish before dusk. Twilight was just beginning as I put away my equipment. I washed and changed. The night shift must've already started because Indulal leaned against the railing of the main deck as I took a walk to dry my hair. I turned away to avoid him, but he'd already noticed me.

"You are troubled today," he pointed out.

"I'm always in trouble."

"That may be so, but today you are *troubled*."

"What do you know? You don't know me."

"I do not, but I see you."

I turned to walk away, not caring to puzzle that one out.

"Anger is a poison, but it is far less damaging than apathy. Life is more than existence. Cherish the blessings of both joy and pain."

"Do you know of pain?"

He nodded seriously. "Indeed, I do. Everyone does. Suffering is a part of life. Some suffer more than others, yet that does not diminish the pain of those who suffer less. If one is to value life, one must appreciate the pain for what it is: an indication of life. Do you value life, Ember?"

His direct question and his calm expression caught me off guard.

"Yes."

He smiled brightly. "I thought so." He walked away, leaving me to my thoughts.

My "apathy" is how I've stayed safe. Whenever Helena discovered I cared for something, she destroyed it. Papa and Pika were the only people I could safely love. Besides, she even separated me from them in the end. Have I really only been existing until now? Am I even safe from her? Is "living" the way Indulal sees it worth the risk?

The hard ice that made up my insides faltered a little and cracked.

I didn't notice Charlie until she put her thumb

between my eyebrows. She had one eye closed and the tip of her tongue stuck out as she rubbed her thumb up and down like she was rubbing off a smudge.

"What are you doing?" I asked her, perplexed.

"Smoothing the worry-wrinkle on your forehead. We age faster here, you know." She stopped and smiled. "Are you all right?"

"I'm fine."

"Do you want to talk about it?"

I opened my mouth to refuse, but Indulal's advice still rang in my ears.

"Do you think people can change?" I asked.

"Change how?"

"Like if you've approached the world and people in one way for so long, and you want to try a different way. Is it possible to change how you see the world?"

She thought about it seriously.

"I think it would be difficult. But if I really want to change, it's possible. Besides, my friends would help me." She smiled without doubt.

I took in her answer. *If I really want to...friends? How would friends help? I don't really have any friends...*

I looked at Charlie's smiling face. *Is Charlie my friend? Can you have a friendship start with one person using the other?*

I stood at an emotional precipice. A dark abyss lay below. I didn't know what was in the abyss, and I was scared. I stepped off the ledge.

"Charlie, I need help."

Her smile faded, and her eyebrows drew together.

"I want to change, but I'm afraid of the consequences." I clenched my jaw. *This is really difficult to admit.*

She stepped forward and caught my eyes. "It's all right. I'm here with you. You don't have to be afraid. What do you want to change?"

I held her eyes like a lifeline. "I want...to care again."

She pulled me into a tight hug. I hesitantly placed my fingertips on her back. She tightened her embrace and didn't seem like she was going to let go anytime soon. I hugged her back softly.

The ice melted a little, so I tightened my embrace with sincerity. I shivered, and the melting ice turned into slush. She loosened her embrace and stared me right in the eyes.

"Of course I'll help you, Ember. Caring will be easier than you think. I'm sure you haven't forgotten how. In fact, it probably takes more effort to suppress emotions since they're completely natural, after all. Expressing those feelings will be much more difficult than simply feeling them."

The thought of vocalizing my feelings often made me shudder.

"Let's just go slowly," I said warily.

She smiled and nodded. "Is this what you were upset about today?"

"No, I wasn't upset today."

She gave me a look.

I sighed. "I was angry that Willie was being rude to Reilley and that Reilley slept out on the main deck to avoid him. Then I was angry at myself for caring."

"See? You already care. You just have to allow yourself to. What did Willie do? He's gruff but not usually mean."

"Apparently, he made Reilley feel bad by comparing him to the previous cook. He said the other cook wasn't so annoying."

Charlie went very still. Her eyes got wide, and she held her breath.

"Are you all right?"

"I'll talk to Willie tomorrow," she said, holding something in. "I'm sorry. I still have to wash tonight. I'll see you later." She walked away abruptly.

As my eyes followed her, my heartbeat echoed in the cavern that is loneliness. I started to smash the unusual feeling down but stopped myself. I let the hollow feeling empty me.

Pain means I'm alive.

I walked to the end of the main deck and took the stairs down to the quarterdeck.

The mess hall was empty except for Reilley cleaning up after the night shift's first meal. He looked up when I entered. His smile was bright, warm, and all the things I usually ran from. I didn't run but nodded at him.

"Ember, I thought you were on the day shift?"

I nodded.

"Aren't you tired? Are you hungry?" he asked.

I shook my head.

"Oh, okay." Thankfully, he didn't ask why I was there. He just kept wiping surfaces.

I sat at one of the tables and watched him work.

After a while, I realized he was humming. He moved with the tune that he had called *Titania*.

"Reilley?"

"Mmm?"

"You told Brewster you worked at an inn with your parents."

"Mmm-hmm," he confirmed.

"Where did you go when it burned down?"

He paused as he cleaned, then started again more slowly. "Umm, I stayed with my aunt, my dad's sister." He tried for matter-of-fact.

"Why aren't you with her now?"

"She got married, and her new husband wanted to start a family, so I left." He struggled to stifle his emotions.

"Did your aunt want you to leave?"

He shrugged.

"What did you tell her?"

"I said I was an adult now, and I wanted to go out and make my own way."

"What happened, Reilley?"

He flinched.

My curiosity is hurting him.

"Umm, what do you mean?"

"Never mind. Don't worry about it."

His shoulders slumped in relief or defeat, I wasn't sure which.

"Hey." I moved behind him as he bent to wipe another table and placed a hand on his shoulder. "I'm glad I found you when I did." I left the mess hall before he could respond.

I returned to my bunk and slept soundly until dawn.

The rest of the week blurred together. Wake up, eat, work, eat, work, et cetera. My emotions were hard to handle since I'd decided to let them flow. My equilibrium was off-kilter, and my mood could shift rapidly. Mostly, everything just felt very intense as my numbing ice melted.

Indulal seemed pleased his speech had had an effect. Charlie tried to be supportive. Whenever my mask slid back into place, she'd poke me in the ribs with her boney finger.

We landed one evening shortly after I'd finished checking the envelope. Since I was done, I went to the cargo hold to help the rest of the deckhands unload. We passed through engineering, which was in a frenzy. The gears were winding the metal coils tightly, and engineering deckhands hauled the coal-like substance in from a hatch in the hull.

Shy directed us on where to move the boxes. I didn't know what was in them, but they were lighter than they looked. We carried them off the ship and placed them in carts. The captain talked with the owner of the carts while Brewster stood by. I thought we'd load another shipment into the hold, but Brewster said it wouldn't arrive until morning. He paid us and dismissed us until then.

I didn't want to waste my pay on food, so I ate in the mess hall. Reilley had to purchase ingredients again, and he asked if he could go ashore with me. Charlie had some repairs to do, but she said she'd join us later. She pulled the ticking disc from her pocket and handed it to me.

"This is a watch. It's five o'clock now. See how the short hand is on the five, and the long hand is on the twelve? Come back to the dock in two hours. I should be finished by then. That will be when the long hand is on the twelve, and the short hand is on the seven. Seven o'clock, got it?"

I nodded and carefully put the watch in my pocket. I stood on the dock waiting for Reilley as Nick, Indulal, Mac, and Sasha disembarked to explore the city.

"Ember," Sasha purred as the others went ahead. "Such a beautiful woman should not have to entertain herself when others could amuse her."

"You want to amuse me, Sasha?"

His eyes glinted, and he nodded.

"What do you have in mind?"

"It is your choice. All I desire is your happiness."

I stepped closer to him. "My happiness?"

"Da." He smiled seductively.

"Then tell me something, Sasha."

"Anything."

"Why do you treat women like you do?"

He answered without hesitation. "Women are beautiful, but they are most beautiful when they know you think them beautiful. Have you ever wanted to live in a work of art? A song or a painting that so moved you that the rest of the world fell away? Every woman is unique with her own passions, fears, colors, and flavors. I discover her and love her in a way that makes her love herself for the work of art she is. I appreciate her for all her beauty, strength, and intelligence. I want to share that appreciation with her if she is willing to be appreciated."

I stared at him. *I was* not *expecting that.*

Sasha stepped into my personal space but didn't touch me.

"Do you want to be appreciated for all of your beauty, strength, and intelligence, Ember?"

Before I could answer, Reilley got my attention. "Ember, are you ready?"

He stood on the dock near us. I had no idea when he'd arrived. Sasha and Reilley both expected an answer from me.

"Sorry, Sasha. I already promised to go with Reilley today."

"Another time?"

"Perhaps." I made no promises.

Reilley looked at Sasha seriously as I passed him to leave the dock. Then he smiled at me brightly as we walked away together.

Sasha's proposal has appeal. I haven't been with a man in some time, not since Duncan. A pang of guilt stabbed at my raw heart. *I'm sure Sasha would be safe, but that would only complicate things right now. Even if we can both participate without attachments, and I'm sure we could, we do work together. We'd have to share that cramped space with the other deckhands, too. It would invite trouble.*

I said goodbye to any hope of physical satisfaction with Sasha. It was the smarter decision; I was sure. But the tension that was always inside me coiled a little tighter.

A flash of memory made me laugh out loud.

Reilley looked at my outburst with a question. "What is it?" He was eager to join in on the joke.

I shook my head and swallowed my laughter. The flash of my boot-dagger on Sasha's neck played in my mind. *I didn't know he was a consent kind of guy then. I never suspected I'd consider his proposal even if I refused in the end. He surprised me with his openness and his approach to women. The human realm certainly has changed since I was here last. I guess they finally learned how to appreciate the differences between the sexes rather than using them against each other.*

6

Reilley and I wandered around the bustling city. He rushed from shop window to food cart, absorbing all the sights, sounds, and smells with enthusiasm. I kept track of our direction so we could find the way back to the dock.

It was difficult to stay aware of our surroundings with so much bombarding my senses. This city was by far the most crowded I'd ever seen. The people ebbed and flowed like water through the current that was the crowd. They forced their way through to wherever they were going. A thick cloud of steam poured from the food stands. The intriguing smells of food mixed with the other city smells of human sweat, sewage, and horse droppings, creating an unappetizing combination.

A woman with a pointed hat approached me and held out a luscious fabric. She chattered at me, and I didn't understand a word. I looked up to see Reilley cheerfully talking with a man in long robes. I tried to move around the woman to get to him. She grabbed my elbow, and I turned an icy glare on her that needed no translation. She let go and moved on to her next target.

I looked toward Reilley again. He and the robed man were gone. I scanned the crowd, but there was no sign of them. My stomach lurched, and I swallowed my panic. I moved as quickly as I could to the place where Reilley had just stood.

To the right was a dim alley with curtained doors lining the sides. I shot into the shady street.

"Reilley?" I called and received no answer.

Up ahead, a curtain covered the light that spilled into the alley. I rushed for that doorway. Ripping open the curtain, I lunged inside.

In the small room, two men sat on crates playing cards on a box in between them. They looked up as I entered.

"Where is he?"

Neither responded as they returned to their game. I spotted a door at the back of the room and barreled toward it. The two men moved to stop me.

"I don't have time for this," I told them as they blocked my way.

The one closest to the door I wanted to get through crossed his thick arms over his chest and lifted his chin, looking down at me with a smirk. His wirier friend stepped toward me and pointed the way I'd come.

"This party is closed," he said with a heavy accent. "If you don't have an invitation, leave."

"I just need to get my friend. Then I'll leave."

He shook his head and grabbed my upper arm to escort me out. "You will leave now."

I rotated my elbow and broke his grip, then pulled back and drove the heel of my hand into his nose.

He let out a grunt and bent with his fingers over his nose. I used his preoccupation to advance toward his larger cohort, but he recovered quickly and kicked me from behind. I stumbled right into the arms of the door guard, who spun me around and pinned my arms behind me.

The smaller man wiped the blood from his upper lip with the back of his hand as he approached me. Before I could escape, he punched me twice in the ribs. I tried not to cry out as pain radiated from my side, but I couldn't stifle the grunts. He stepped back, satisfied with his retaliation.

I sagged, trying to fall to the floor, but the man behind me held me up, putting strength in his arms. I used his force to lift my feet and kick the man in front of me. He flew back and hit his head on the far wall.

The man who held me dropped me in surprise and ran forward to check on his friend. As he knelt, I grabbed a bottle from the box they'd been playing cards on and cracked it over his head. He crumbled atop his comrade.

I hissed as I touched my side where I'd been punched and knew I'd be bruised later. The door ahead led to a dark hallway, which ended in a set of creaky stairs.

I flew down the stairs and hit a solid door. I

kicked it open and was not expecting what I found. The room was not dark and dingy, but warmly lit. Plush cushions and shimmering drapes accommodated men and women in all states of undress.

I scanned the writhing bodies for Reilley's blond head. He wasn't there.

A doorway at the other end of the room had me walking deeper into the den. I kept my eyes on my goal and tried to ignore the sounds of pleasure.

Through the doorway was a hallway that ended in an elegant door. I approached the door and opened it boldly and without ceremony.

Reilley lay flat on his back on a large bed with his arms and legs spread wide. A sleek woman straddled his waist. She was unbuttoning his shirt, but his pants were still on.

Oh shit, did I just interrupt Reilley at a bad time?

The woman turned her silky head in my direction. Reilley didn't move.

"Who are you? Get out of here!" she demanded haughtily.

Reilley still didn't move.

"Reilley!" I snapped.

No response.

Oh gods. I rushed to the bed.

The woman did not like being ignored, but she didn't like me approaching more. She turned red with fury. "Get out of here now, or I'll..." She clipped her threat with my dagger at her throat.

"You'll what?" I dared her to finish.

She paled.

My heart jumped into my throat when I looked down at Reilley. His eyes were closed, and his jaw was slack. I sighed with relief when I saw his chest moving up and down as he breathed.

"Is there another way out of here?" I asked the pretty rapist.

She pointed to one of the doors on the far side of the room. I nodded and punched her in her polished face. She went down and was out. Her nose bled on her luscious cream gown.

Pain shot through my hand and wrist. I grasped my injury with my other hand and clenched my teeth, sucking in air. I screamed all manner of obscenities in my head, but it was my own fault. *Okay. Punching someone in the face with a closed fist isn't the best idea, but it was worth it.* I beat down the anger I felt at myself for allowing her to make it personal and basked in the glory of her broken face.

Resheathing my dagger, which I'd dropped while clutching my injury, I leaned down to Reilley.

"Reilley?"

No response.

I slapped his face lightly.

Nothing.

This is going to be difficult.

I grabbed Reilley's ankles and pulled his legs off the bed. My hand throbbed in protest, but I worked through the pain. I pulled his arms until he sat on the edge. I knelt and hauled him onto my back, wrapping his arms around my neck. His feet dragged behind me as I carried him through the escape door.

The door led to a dark hallway, which led to another door. Lucky for us, that door took us directly outside. Leaving an alley, we entered another crowded street. I scanned the street to get my bearings and find a way back to the airship.

On one side of the street was a pub with tables on the sidewalk. The tables were packed with rowdy drinkers. A flicker of fiery-red hair in the sea of black caught my eye.

Mac, Indulal, Nick, and Sasha sat at a table, drinking. I trudged toward them.

"Mac!" I called desperately.

He didn't hear me over the sounds of the city.

I waded into the crowd toward him, shouldering people out of the way. I continued to call to Mac, but he didn't hear me until I stood next to him. He looked up at me as he lowered his drink.

"Ember, what—" He started, eyes wide.

A ruckus came from the other side of the street. Everyone looked in that direction. The two men who'd been guarding the den had awoken and presumably come looking for me. I turned my back to them, and Reilley's superior height hid me from view.

"Mac, we need to get back to the airship now."

"Right."

He didn't miss a beat. He threw Reilley over his shoulder with ease, and we all made our escape.

I followed Mac closely and passed through the crowd with little effort as it parted for his solid form. Sasha, Nick, and Indulal were not far behind us.

We got to the docks much faster than I could've managed alone. Searching behind me, I saw we'd lost our pursuers. Charlie waited impatiently for us at the dock. She took in Reilley draped over Mac.

"What happened?" she asked worriedly.

"Charlie, fetch Smitty," Mac directed.

Charlie dashed off, and Mac carried Reilley through the hatch to the cargo hold. We proceeded to the mess hall on the quarterdeck. Charlie met us there with a broad-shouldered man from engineering.

Mac busted open the door to Reilley's bunk. Willie wasn't there. Mac laid Reilley in his cot gently, and Smitty knelt next to him.

"What happened?" Smitty demanded, checking Reilley's pulse.

Everyone else looked at me.

"I don't know. He was there one second and gone the next. I found him like this under a woman who was undressing him."

Smitty opened Reilley's eyelids and looked at his eyes.

"You two," Smitty pointed at Charlie and me, "turn your backs."

Unsure as to why that was necessary, I faced the door. I heard a zipping sound.

"All right," Smitty gave us permission to look again. "Someone slipped him a cherry."

Charlie gasped, and Mac nodded. I looked to Charlie for an explanation; she made a motion as if to say, "later."

"He'll be fine, but he'll have quite a headache when he wakes in a few hours," Smitty continued. "I'll bring some painkillers." Smitty left.

"Reilley was on ingredient duty?" Mac asked me.

I nodded.

"I'll find Willie and tell him to take care of it." Mac left.

I crossed the small room and knelt next to Reilley. "What's a cherry, Charlie?"

She moved closer to me and answered softly. "Cherry is the street name for a drug. It's used to make people, particularly men, fall asleep. Most often, it's used for sexual assault."

I clenched my teeth. "Why do you say particularly men?"

"It has a unique symptom: it keeps men erect through many ejaculations."

Despair soured my stomach. "Why would someone do this?" I choked around the lump in my throat.

Charlie put a comforting arm around me. "I don't know. The rapid nature of what you described makes it sound like that woman is well practiced at cherry picking. Reilley was very lucky to have you there, Ember," she soothed. She stood and moved to the door. "I'm going to see if Willie needs any help getting ingredients."

I knelt by Reilley and watched him breathe, taking comfort in the rising and falling of his bare chest. Thinking of that smooth woman undressing him, I carefully rebuttoned his shirt. Smitty entered and held up a pouch of powder.

"Dissolve this in water and make him drink it when he wakes," he directed and offered me the pouch.

Without thinking, I reached out with my injured hand. Smitty took in my bloody knuckles and swollen wrist.

"Let me see your hand," he ordered.

"I'm all right," I reassured him with confidence.

He stared at me with a hard, unyielding gaze. Realizing I wouldn't win, I offered him my hand. He took it gently in his rough, calloused hands. He explored the extent of my injuries with a tender prodding.

"Well, it isn't broken, but your wrist is sprained. I'll get supplies."

I knelt by Reilley and waited for Smitty to return. He didn't take long. He cleaned my cuts with a stinging liquid and wrapped a long bandage around my hand and wrist. Then he handed me a glass of water.

"Drink this. I've dissolved a painkiller and an anti-inflammatory in it. Try not to overuse that wrist, and it should be all right in a few weeks."

Smitty stayed just long enough to make sure I drank all of the bitter water.

I returned to Reilley. He slept peacefully, and I was there to make sure. Each exhale made me sigh in relief. The terror I'd felt while frantically searching for him and then trying to get him to safety slipped away and left a foggy exhaustion. Each hot breath melted my stomach slush until there was only cold water. I stared at his face until it was etched in my mind's eye. I realized the bruises he had from when we first met were nearly gone. *He must be using the witch hazel.* I smiled inwardly. Watching him so closely made him seem otherworldly.

The shifting of weight on the cot had me jumping up and shaking sleep from my head. Reilley groaned and placed a hand on his head while trying to sit. I rushed to help him, placing my hand behind his back and assisting him.

"Reilley, are you all right? Does your head hurt?"

"Mmm," he confirmed.

"Hold on, I'll get you some medicine." I snatched the pouch of powder Smitty had given me, ran to the kitchen, filled a glass with water, and stirred in the powder. Returning to his bunk, I gently wrapped his fingers around the glass.

"Here, drink this. It'll make you feel better." I moved his hand toward his mouth and made sure he drank the whole glass. After taking the cup, I placed it beside the cot.

"Ember? Where am I?" he mumbled.

"We're in your bunk on the airship. Do you remember anything?"

"I remember a robed man offering me something to drink. He said it was a gift from his mistress."

"Reilley, why would you take food from strangers?" I censured softly.

"He said it was really sweet, and it was rude in their culture to refuse gifts."

I harrumphed.

"What happened?" he asked, finally opening his eyes and squinting at the light.

I stared at him seriously.

"She was a cherry picker," I repeated what Charlie said, hoping he'd understand.

His puzzled expression wanted more information.

"That man drugged you so his mistress could take advantage of you."

He looked down at his erection. "Oh." His face turned pale, and he lay back on his cot. "How did I get here then?"

"I followed your snatcher and stopped her before anything happened. Then I dragged you out and happened to find Mac. He carried you back here."

"So she didn't...take advantage of me?"

"No."

He sighed in relief. "Thank you, Ember." His voice cracked, and tears started to leak from his eyes.

I wiped his tears and smiled gently. "I'm glad I found you."

A knock at the door alerted us to a visitor. I opened it and saw the captain and Mr. Brewster waiting to enter. The captain's direct eyes demanded attention.

"Ember, is it?" she asked.

"Yes, Ma'am."

She extended her hand and placed it on my shoulder.

"Well done, Ember. Your crewmate is home safe because of you." Her gratitude hit me in the gut.

I nodded. "Captain."

She moved around me and crossed the room to Reilley, who was trying to stand.

"Rest easy, Reilley," she said.

He settled for sitting.

"How are you faring?" she asked him.

Grabbing my attention, Mr. Brewster motioned me into the mess hall.

"We know what happened, in general, but please give me the details."

I related the misadventure to him with all the particulars. He nodded, taking mental notes. Then he asked specifics about the location of the den and the appearances of the robed man, the woman, and the doormen.

When I was finished, he looked at me directly. "You did well."

"Thank you, Sir."

The captain exited the bunks, and Brewster went in to see Reilley. I waited outside to give them privacy.

7

I sat at a table in the mess hall when Willie returned. He strode with purpose toward the bunks with his teeth clenched and his eyes glaring.

"Mr. Brewster is in there," I informed him.

He stopped in his tracks and marched to the kitchen, grumbling to himself. After a few minutes of him slamming kitchen equipment, I popped up and stomped to him.

"Reilley will be sleeping in his own cot from now on," I ordered.

"I didn't tell the runt to move bunks," Willie shot back.

I bristled at what he'd called Reilley. "It was still your doing."

He grunted without remorse.

"You're lucky to have a crewmate like him. He does his job well and doesn't complain. You couldn't ask for anyone better."

He spun on me. "What do you know, Girl? Everything was fine before you and the runt arrived.

I got no notice when Johnny left. He just disappeared, and Charlie is off pretending he never existed rather than telling me where he went or going to find him. Not to mention, I had no say in his replacement. You can bet I wouldn't have chosen that runt. Now, I have to share my space with a cheery half-wit."

I glared and stepped in close to Willie. "Call him a runt or a half-wit one more time, and you'll disappear as cleanly as your pal Johnny," I promised in a quiet growl.

His hackles rose, and he opened his mouth to respond. He must've seen the sincerity in my expression because he tramped from the room without another word.

Mr. Brewster exited Reilley's bunk and approached me.

"Smitty tells me you were injured. Will you be able to work?"

"I think so," I responded, distracted.

"All right. Well, don't push yourself too hard, and take breaks if you need to."

I nodded, and Brewster left. I beat down my anger at Willie and returned to Reilley.

"Hey," I said softly, kneeling by his cot. "How're you doing?"

He smiled at me. "I'm fine, Ember. The medicine helped my headache. Now, I'm just tired. But I still have to go get ingredients."

"Willie already got them, so you should just rest."

"That was nice of him."

"Yeah..." I muttered.

He gasped, and I jumped.

"What is it? Are you all right?" I asked frantically.

"What happened to your hand?" he demanded, his voice rising in panic.

"Oh," I sighed. "My wrist is just sprained."

His worried eyes watered as he searched my face. I reassured him with a small smile, and he relaxed a little.

"Hey, you must be hungry. There's a food stall pretty close to the dock. Do you want me to go get something good?"

"I am kind of hungry."

"Okay. I'll be right back."

Walking to the cargo hold, I started to evaluate my conversation with Willie.

So Johnny was the previous cook Reilley said Willie compared him to, but what does that have to do with Charlie? Willie did seem upset by the whole thing. They must've been friends.

Before I could feel too sorry for him, I remembered how much of an ass he was.

After disembarking, I walked to the nearest food cart. I bought whatever smelled good, chunks of fried fish on a stick. Returning to the dock, I heard a muffled whispering coming from around the side of the ship. The guard, who should've been posted, wasn't around. Curious, I inched closer when I heard voices.

"I don't think I can pull thirty without someone noticing. How about fifteen?" a voice said.

"We need thirty," another voice responded.

"I don't know what to tell you. They're in high demand. It's fifteen or none."

"Fine, but they better be in pristine condition."

"Yeah, yeah. Just be at the drop point on time."

Footsteps sounded, heading in the direction I was standing. I scrambled through the hatch and rushed through the cargo hold back to Reilley's bunk.

Handing Reilley the fried fish nuggets, I ate mine quietly and thought about what I'd just heard.

It sounds like someone is embezzling cargo and selling it for individual profit. I wonder if it's someone on our ship or another ship docked here.

"That was delicious. Thank you, Ember." Reilley yawned and tried to fight his heavy lids.

"You should probably get some sleep."

"Do you think Willie will mind if I stay here tonight?"

"Don't worry about Willie. It's your bunk, too."

He yawned again and settled into his cot. I took his skewer and his water glass.

"See you tomorrow," I said.

"Goodnight, Ember."

I threw away the sticks and washed and put away the glass. On my way out of the kitchen, Shy stopped me.

"Hey, Ember, how's Reilley? Is he awake yet?"

"He was, but he should be asleep again."

"Okay. I thought he might be hungry, so I brought him a snack." He indicated to the small cardboard box he carried.

"He just ate. You can leave it for him."

"Oh? Did you cook?"

I snorted at his joke. "I got fried fish from a food cart."

"That cart by the dock? That place is great." He pulled out a pen and wrote a note on the box, then left it near Reilley's door. "Well, goodnight then." He waved as he headed to the cargo hold.

Relieved that this horrid day was over, I washed and headed to my own bunk. Charlie was reading alone, like the day we first met.

"How's Reilley?" she asked, putting her book down.

"He's resting now. I think he'll be all right."

"And are you all right?"

I went to brush off her inquiry, but her eyes, clouded with sincere concern, made me answer truthfully.

"I'm relieved nothing happened, but mostly angry. What kind of people would do this? Is this what humans are like?"

"Far worse things have happened in Faerie," she said with a deadpan voice and far away expression.

I nodded in agreement.

"How's your wrist?"

"I should be fine if I don't go too fast."

Pleasantries over, I wanted to ask about Johnny.

"Charlie, Willie and I had a conversation."

"Oh yeah? I talked to him, too. I think he'll be better with Reilley in the future, so don't worry."

"Did he talk to you about our conversation?"

"No, he didn't mention it." She shrugged.

"He talked about how he didn't get a choice in hiring Reilley. He also mentioned the previous cook."

"Oh really? That's interesting. Well, all this excitement has me beat. I'm sure you're tired, too. Goodnight."

She snuffed out the light and the conversation.

The next morning, my body was stiff and sore. My torso was bruised from my fight with the doormen, and my wrist ached.

Reilley was back in the kitchen, cooking breakfast. Willie was grumpy and avoided eye contact with me.

"How're you feeling, Reilley?" I asked while grabbing a plate.

"I'm much better after I slept. How're you?"

"I'm fine." A twinge of pain echoed in the wake of my lie. *Should I get more powder from Smitty?*

I sat next to Charlie. The rest of the deckhands were loading cargo so we could weigh anchor. Charlie seemed distracted this morning and not in the mood to talk, so I ate quietly beside her.

After breakfast, I went to work. I was attempting to put my gear on, but my wrist couldn't bend right. Frustrated, I growled at myself.

"May I help?"

I looked up at Sasha's solicitous expression. I searched his face for signs that he thought me weak and found none. I gave him a short nod, and he stepped closer.

He didn't ask if I was capable of working, and his face held no judgment. I soaked in the beauty of his movements as he fixed my twisted harness. His body heat lit me up, and my inner coil wound tighter, ready to break. Like a dancer, he was strong and graceful. He moved slower than necessary as he fastened the harness in front. Letting the buckle strap slip through his fingers, his light eyes slid to mine.

I didn't hide my appreciation as I stared boldly back.

A throat cleared, and I looked around Sasha to see Reilley standing with a napkin-wrapped biscuit. He met my eyes, then blushed and looked away. My stomach dropped, seeing the flustered look Reilley wore. My instinct was to step out of Sasha's reach and toward Reilley to comfort him. What that instinct could mean made me nervous. I locked that compulsion down and stood my ground. Rolling right over why that was my compulsion into why I wouldn't step away, I clenched my teeth.

If he wants to be around me, he needs to get used to these types of situations. I'm not going to pursue Sasha, but I'm not dead either.

Feeling like I'd convinced myself, I nodded. "Reilley," I said coldly.

His face red and eyes downcast, he handed me the napkin. "I just came to bring you a snack. Be careful today." He rushed away.

Turning back to Sasha, I faced his discerning gaze. His cool eyes analyzed my reaction to Reilley's response. I looked away, not wanting to face my reflection.

"Where is your heart, Ember? I can make you feel amazing, true. But I think you will not come to me. The boy appreciates you. Why you do not appreciate him?"

I stuffed the napkin into my belt and headed for the ladder. Pulling my goggles into place, I gingerly tested my wrist to see if it could hold me. It could if I was careful and didn't twist it. Sasha watched me closely as I tugged the rope twice and ascended the envelope.

My work was slow-going. Hearing the lunch bell, I climbed down and went to the mess hall.

Reilley still wouldn't meet my eyes as I grabbed a plate, but I could feel his eyes on me when I sat with Sasha, Mac, and Charlie. I ignored my flushed face and stifled the shame I felt for being so mean to Reilley.

"How're you holding up, Ember?" Mac asked.

"It's a little slow. I'm not sure I'll finish before sunset."

"Don't stress too much. If that happens, mark your spot and start there tomorrow."

I nodded in assent.

I asked Charlie to help me with my harness. She still seemed melancholy, so I didn't pester her with unnecessary chatter. Besides, I had my own problems.

I wasn't finished as twilight settled in. Determined to complete the section I was on, I checked the fabric as I rappelled.

As I braced my knees on the metal frame and ran my hands over the fabric, the trusted rope that held my weight and kept me securely suspended shuddered. I gasped and my heart hammered my chest like it was an anvil as I fell a few inches before the rope stiffened again.

I couldn't hear my heavy breaths over the wind in my ears. Clutching the rope with my injured hand, I fumbled into my tool belt for the tin whistle.

I let out a relieved sigh as my trembling fingers found its cold, smooth surface. Holding it with my fingertips, I pulled it gently from my tool belt. I licked my lips and brought my shaking hand toward my mouth.

As my injured hand felt the rope vibrate, I flinched and the whistle slipped through my fingers. It glinted in the setting sun as it plunged toward the ground far below.

Fuck.

Looking around desperately, I saw the emergency access ladder about a foot out of reach. I took a deep breath and released it all at once. I tried to inch toward it, but the rope above me seemed to be stuck on something.

I carefully pushed myself out until I was standing. As I reached for the ladder, the rope shuddered again. Gritting my teeth, I kicked myself hard to the side just as the rope above me let loose and sent me into a free fall.

My injured wrist screamed as my hand gripped the rope ladder. I trembled as I clung to the side of the envelope, taking a few deep breaths to calm myself.

Looking up, I saw something flapping on the top of the envelope. I climbed toward it, worried the fabric was torn.

Reaching the summit, I realized the flapping fabric was the tail of Shy's coat. He stood by the reel as if waiting for me.

"I should've known you wouldn't make this easy."

"You," I accused as he pulled a pipe from his

inside jacket pocket and moved toward me. I hadn't known it was him, but I wasn't terribly surprised either.

"You just couldn't mind your own business, could you?" he sighed at me, disappointed.

I crouched into a fighting stance, far more balanced on the top of the envelope than he.

"Guess not," I mocked.

He angled for an opening and swung. I dodged.

"I wonder if riggers are born too curious for their own good or if the job makes you that way. I saw you scurry away after listening in last night."

"I'd say it's your sloppiness and stupidity that gets you caught," I taunted.

He growled, swung, and missed.

"So how long have you been stealing from the ship?" I asked nonchalantly, like we were having tea rather than him trying to kill me.

"Long enough to know you were trouble right away."

"I'm not trouble. We're just good friends."

"It does seem that way. I find people rely too much on machines these days. It's only a matter of time before there's an accident. Don't be too sad. Your little buddy will be joining you soon."

"Reilley doesn't know anything." Panic tainted my voice.

"I can't be sure of that. Anyway, he'll ask too many questions."

I forced my eyes wide and furrowed my brow. I held my hands up defensively and backed away from him. He advanced on his scared prey, smiling in victory. He raised the pipe over his head with both arms, readying for one strong blow.

I crouched as if cowering, using the farced gesture to reach for my boot-dagger. One strike. He looked down at his chest in shock, my dagger hilt embedded in his black heart.

Without a word, I kicked him in the chest and sent him flying off the envelope and toward the ground far below.

Damn it. I liked that dagger.

Climbing down in the dark was difficult. All the deckhands, along with the captain and Mr. Brewster waited on the main deck.

"Ember, my quarters," the captain ordered as my feet landed.

I nodded and followed her. Mr. Brewster brought up the rear. Everyone in engineering watched as we passed.

"Ember!" Reilley called out, worried, as I passed the mess hall.

I held up my hand to silence him and gave him a small smile for reassurance.

We entered the captain's quarters, and she took a seat behind a solid table. Mr. Brewster guarded the only door.

"Well?" the captain demanded.

"The short version: Shy thought I knew he was embezzling cargo. He tried to kill me to keep me quiet. I tried to kill him right back, only I succeeded. Also, it seems he killed the previous rigger for the same reason."

She nodded. "So it was Shy," she said grimly.

I was surprised she believed me, but she sounded

like she knew someone had been skimming the goods. She sat silently, thinking for a while.

Finally, she turned serious eyes on me. "Tell me the details."

I told her how I'd overhead someone, how I was attacked, that he threatened Reilley, and everything else.

"It's unfortunate that we don't know his accomplice on the ground. Also, he should've faced legal justice, but I understand it was self-defense. I'll take care of the rest. Do you need to see Smitty?"

My wrist throbbed and my side hurt when I breathed, but I shook my head. "Captain, I did notice the guard was gone when I overheard Shy talking to his buyer."

"That may be related. I'll look into it. You're dismissed."

Mr. Brewster stepped away from the door and let me pass.

Reilley ambushed me as I passed the mess hall.

"Ember, are you all right?" He clutched my shoulders, and his eyes raked my body for injuries.

"I'm fine." I smiled gently and placed my hand on his, glad for a chance to show kindness after being mean earlier. He seemed unconvinced at first and continued to look me over. Finally, he sighed in relief.

I explained to him what had happened, leaving out Shy's threat to kill him. He was rattled and kept staring at me as if to prove I was all right. Tired, I tried to say goodnight and go to my bunk.

"Wait." Reilley grabbed my uninjured hand. "I'm worried about you being alone."

"I won't be alone. The day shift deckhands will be with me."

"But I won't be there."

I was amused but touched that he wanted to protect me when he couldn't protect himself.

"I'm just going to sleep. Charlie is there too," I reassured him.

He reluctantly released my arm, and I went toward my bunk.

All the deckhands waited on the main deck to hear what had happened. I told the short version and excused myself so I could sleep. Charlie, Sasha, and Mac entered the bunks with me. We were all exhausted, but that didn't stop them from being overly solicitous about my health. I was glad when the light was finally extinguished. I slept soundly and awoke rested though still sore.

Reilley watched me carefully at breakfast, like I'd disappear if he took his eyes off me. I heard Willie scold him for burning the eggs.

After breakfast, I waited on the main deck as an engineer finished fixing the reel. It seemed that Shy hadn't sabotaged the machine as much as pressed the release button. It didn't take the engineer too long to attach another rope.

As I stood by, I pulled Charlie aside.

"Charlie, are you all right? You've seemed down the last few days."

Her face softened. "Ember, you really have started to care, haven't you?"

I wasn't going to let her deflect this time. "Partially because of you, but I have a long way to go. Please tell me what's bothering you."

"I will. I just need time to think it through."

"Isn't that something friends should do together?"

She smiled sadly. "Sometimes, it's a personal thing that one has to work out alone."

Reluctantly, I bowed to her will.

"I'll talk to you when I figure it out."

Charlie helped me with my harness and sent me on my way. This time, I waited for Reilley to bring me a biscuit. After a while, I couldn't wait anymore, so I started to finish my inspection from the day before.

I squashed the disappointment I felt that Reilley hadn't come.

It's not like he promised. He just always does. It's incredible how just a few weeks can make something habitual. Maybe he didn't have time. Maybe he couldn't get away.

My stomach bottomed out.

Maybe he's hurt.

I tried to convince myself that it wasn't the case and something had just come up. But worry ruined my concentration. I rappelled down immediately to find Reilley. Without removing my equipment, I rushed to the mess hall. I did a quick sweep and didn't see anyone. I ran to his bunk and banged on the door in a panic.

"Reilley!"

I know he's on day shift.

Reaching for the door handle, I was going in.

"Ember?" Reilley stood behind the kitchen counter, pulling biscuits from the oven.

My heart raced as relief flooded my system.

"I'm sorry the biscuits weren't ready before you left."

I removed my hat and wiped my forehead with the back of my forearm. I sighed out the breath I didn't know I'd been holding and removed my fogged goggles to see him better.

He stared at me wide-eyed and dropped the cookie sheet on the floor. Biscuits rolled as the metal crashed. I rushed to him to figure out what was wrong.

"Are you all right? Did you get burned?"

He continued to stare, mouth agape.

Grabbing his hands, I examined them. *They don't look burned.*

With a look of fascination, Reilley lifted his hand toward me slowly. He moved like someone trying not to spook a scared animal. I was taken aback by his expression and the cautious way he reached for me.

Making contact, he ran his fingertips lightly along the ridge of my right ear from point to lobe. A shiver of pleasure ran down my spine. It was quickly smashed by the horrifying realization that Reilley had seen my ears, my only obviously Fae feature.

I stepped out of his reach and quickly rearranged my hair. Then I jammed my hat back into place.

His wonder turned to shame.

"I'm sorry, Ember. I should've asked first," he whispered.

"Reilley...do you know what this means?" I asked, trying to gauge his understanding.

His eyes lit up all sparkly, and he smiled. He nodded slowly. "Oh yes, my mother used to tell me stories. You're a f—"

I stopped the word with my fingertips on his mouth.

"Don't say it."

My sudden proximity made him blush.

"Reilley," I whispered urgently. "You can't tell anyone. It could put me in more danger."

His embarrassment was swept away by alarm. "Danger? What kind of danger?"

I answered him seriously. "Potentially the fatal kind."

His expression showed he understood the gravity of keeping this secret.

"What can I do to keep you safe?" he asked with a seriousness I didn't know he had.

"Just don't tell anyone."

He stared down at me, his green eyes like deep pools of jade. "I'll never tell anyone. I will protect you."

My mind blurred in response. Astonished by Reilley's solemn oath, my thoughts scrambled, trying to reconcile what I knew of Reilley and what I was witnessing.

How can someone who can't take care of himself protect me? But I can't bring myself to laugh it off. He's serious about this. As long as he doesn't tell anyone, that's enough.

"Thank you, Reilley," I said gratefully.

He gave me a slow nod. I blinked, and the old Reilley was back.

"I'm sorry about the biscuits." He knelt and started to pick them up off the floor. "Oh, did you come down here looking for me?" He looked up, curious.

My face grew warm, and I bit my lower lip. "Uh, yes. Have you seen Charlie?"

"Not since breakfast. Do you want help looking for her?"

"No, it's not that important. I'll catch her later. I better get back to work."

"Wait. I'll get you a snack."

"Don't worry about it," I called over my shoulder as I exited the mess hall.

I returned to the envelope and worked as quickly as my injuries would allow. I was grateful that I had to concentrate to move safely. It allowed me to turn off all the other thoughts flying around in my head.

The lunch bell rang before long, so I carefully climbed down to the main deck. Distracted, I went to the equipment room to hang up my equipment. My harness was much easier to remove than put on with my injured wrist. I opened the door to head to the mess hall.

My body froze in shock as cold water drenched me from head to toe. I looked up and saw Nick on the roof, holding an overturned bucket. A playful grin made his eyes twinkle.

I narrowed my eyes. His grin slipped a little as he tried to gauge my reaction.

"I guess this round goes to you." I bowed to him in honor of his achievement. "Of course, you realize this means war."

His grin widened. "I wouldn't have it any other way."

Finally, he burst into a triumphant laugh. Its infectious nature had me chuckling, too.

After it died out, I looked back up at him. "Seriously, couldn't you have waited until after I did laundry? I don't have any more clean clothes."

"Well, I had to take advantage of your injury.

When would I have a better chance to get the drop on you?"

I grunted in response.

"Could you at least get Charlie to bring me a towel and a pair of my less dirty pants? Also, ask her if she can loan me a shirt."

He nodded. "I'm feeling generous."

I squished to the bathroom.

Removing my wet clothes, I wrung them out and waited for Charlie to bring me a towel. A knock sounded on the door behind me.

"Come in," I called.

The door opened and closed. I turned to thank Charlie for bringing me clothes, but she wasn't the one who entered.

Sasha stood comfortably by the closed door as if I wasn't naked.

"Nick said you asked for me?"

Of course he did.

I just stood there and stared at him. He stared back, trying to maintain his nonchalant expression. His light eyes met mine, and I remembered the feel of his hands on my hips and thighs. The tight coil, so wound up inside me, twisted one time too many and burst.

"Sasha," I whispered.

"Da, Ember," he purred.

"Show me how you would appreciate me."

Consent given, Sasha let his composure slip. He didn't have a look of pure adoration as that would assume he wasn't my equal. His expression, as he moved slowly toward me, was one of confidence and recognition. I felt naked under his smoldering stare, like much more than skin was exposed. His appraisal told me I was worthy of any happiness I could ever want.

I finally understood how ice could burn as his blue eyes made me feverish.

By the time he reached me, I was already hot with anticipation. He moved in slowly and bent down. His lips hovered close to mine as he gauged my commitment one more time. I smiled and tilted my face up to him.

His kiss was thorough and scorching. My bones melted.

Sasha's appreciation did indeed make the world fall away. His attentions made me feel beautiful and strong and revel in this one moment of my life.

He watched me carefully as he discovered what I liked best, exploring all of my colors and flavors. His lips, tongue, and teeth knew exactly where to go and how much pressure was necessary to make me throb and squirm.

Pushing my hair aside and trailing kisses and nibbles down my neck, he only paused shortly as he saw my pointed ear. Then he licked it from lobe to tip, making me shiver. He whispered words of endearment in a language I couldn't understand, but they filled me with warmth nonetheless.

When my knees got too wobbly to support my own weight, he wrapped his arms around my torso to hold me up. That was when he dipped his head to my breasts. I let my head fall back to give him better access, clutching his thick arms for stability.

My head grew heavy and my mind foggy under his mouth's attentions to my tight nipples. One of his hands reached down to my bottom, grasped it firmly and lifted me off my feet.

I wrapped my legs around his waist as he lifted his lips to mine. He strode a few steps and sat me on the cabinet.

Easing his hips away from mine, he reestablished eye contact before removing his shirt over his head. His dark hair was gently mussed.

His pale skin gleamed in the dim light and stretched over muscles that proclaimed his profession. He smiled as he watched me appreciate him. Having taken him in by sight, I reached for him, needing flesh on flesh.

I trailed my fingertips down his torso and made short work of the buttons of his pants. Angling my good wrist, I slipped my hand into his pants and wrapped my fingers around his stiff cock. A shudder ran through him, and his lips returned to mine.

Before long, he knelt before me and spread my thighs. Anticipation built as he slowly kissed my feet and legs. Finally, his mouth showed me humans have a magic all their own.

Having kept quiet throughout the encounter, I couldn't hold in the moan that his tongue elicited.

The fire in my core demanded stoking. As he stood, I yanked at the waist of his pants. They fell to his ankles. Grasping his hips, I pulled him closer. Before I could encase him, he pulled a small packet from his pocket and rolled something onto his erection.

That done, he let me guide his blunt tip into me. He eased in slowly to see how much I could take.

Finding a rhythm, we soon burst together in a sweet and sweaty groan.

Encircling me, Sasha rested his head on my shoulder. I reached up to pet his head, and he trailed kisses up my neck. Pushing my hair back, he stopped at a spot behind my ear.

"What does this symbol mean?" he asked, curious.

"What symbol?"

"This tattoo behind your ear."

"What tattoo?" I asked, still foggy.

"There is a tattoo behind your ear. It looks like a knot with many crossings and loops." He chuckled at me for forgetting my own tattoo.

Confusion turned to panic.

I don't have a tattoo.

Seeing my response, Sasha tried to calm me, running his hands soothingly over my shoulders and arms.

"There are many like you where we are going. Perhaps, one of them can help you. Do not worry until then, da?"

His clear eyes and reassuring expression made me relax and nod. I was peaceful, and the coil inside me was looser than it had been in a long time. After holding each other for a while, Sasha practically begged to be allowed to wash me. He did so carefully and with reverence. He gently washed away the sweat and fluids while caressing me in some places and tickling me in others. I giggled freely, and he smiled and chuckled with me.

He washed himself as well. The rolled bag Sasha

had put on himself had caught all of his seed. I watched him remove it with fascination.

Humans really are brilliant. Now, I don't have to go to an apothecary for tea.

Realizing my clothes were still wet, Sasha let me borrow his shirt and went to fetch me pants and a shirt for him.

"We missed lunch," he said, handing me my pants.

"Maybe I can ask Reilley for a small snack. I'm really hungry."

Clean and dressed, we headed to the mess hall to beg for food.

9

As we entered the deserted mess hall, Reilley looked up from cleaning.

"Ember, I was worried when you didn't come for lunch. I was just about to—" He cut himself off abruptly and stared at me hard.

Though Sasha and I kept a professional distance, I felt relaxed, and I'm sure it showed. My sexual hunger satisfied, I was content and comfortable in my own skin.

Reilley frowned, squinting his eyes slightly.

"Reilley..." I said softly. I smiled at him gently and established eye contact. "I'm sorry I worried you. Sasha and I got into something and lost track of time."

"You're supposed to break for meals. Mr. Brewster said Captain doesn't want us overworked."

"We weren't working, Reilley," I whispered. Sasha nodded sympathetically as Reilley tried to grasp the situation.

Finally, he widened his gaze to include Sasha.

He took in our satiated demeanors. Then his eyes fixed on my shirt, which was Sasha's.

"Did something happen to your clothes?"

"They got wet."

"You don't have more?"

Reilley's voice wavered as he grasped for anything but the truth.

"Sasha let me borrow his."

"That was nice of him."

My chest tightened in the face of Reilley's reaction. I looked to Sasha to see if he had a way to defuse the situation. He stepped closer and placed a supportive hand on my shoulder.

Reilley observed this gesture and my lack of retaliation. His eyes filled with tears, but he refused to let them spill.

"Please excuse me," he whispered. Then he ran from the room toward the cargo hold.

I told Sasha I would talk to Reilley, and he should just go back to work. I went to cargo in search of Reilley. I heard him sniffling and moved in that direction.

"Don't come closer," he called before I could see him.

"Reilley..."

"Go away."

I lost my patience. "This is ridiculous. Why are you being like this? It's not that big of a deal."

"How isn't it?"

"How *is* it? So what? Sasha and I had sex, and?"

He let a little sob escape at my blunt statement. "He must be very special to you. Are you in love with him?"

I sighed. "Sex isn't always about loving someone. Sometimes, it's just sex. We knew there was no room for attachments before starting."

"I don't think that's possible."

"What?"

"How could Sasha not love you? You're wonderful."

I smiled. "That's very nice of you to say, Reilley, but I'm sure Sasha meets many wonderful people. Besides, what makes you think I'm in love with him?"

"I don't know," he mumbled. "He's strong and good looking."

"True, but there are many men like that. It's not so special. Sasha is fun, but he couldn't stand by me for a lifetime."

Reilley peeked his head around the boxes he'd been hiding behind. I pulled my handkerchief from my pocket and wiped the tears from his face. He closed his eyes and leaned into my hand.

"I'll stand by you, Ember," he whispered.

I smiled at him gently. *I'll walk with you until you can walk on your own or until you find someone to walk with. With your sweet personality, it won't be long before some nice woman lays claim to you.*

He responded with a sad smile when I didn't answer.

"Now, we better get back to work," I said.

He nodded.

We returned to our respective jobs, and I finished inspecting the envelope from the day before.

I went back to my bunk to grab my laundry before dinner. Nick and Indulal slept in their cots before the night shift. I was gathering my clothes when Nick whispered, "I told you I was feeling generous."

I threw my pillow at him, and he laughed heartily. The launderers were in a room on the engineering deck. I gave my clothes to a young man, who tagged my bag and gave me a numbered ticket.

"Come back tomorrow afternoon," he said.

I was so hungry when the dinner bell rang, I practically ran to the mess hall. I smiled at Reilley as I took a plate and sat next to Charlie. Sasha sat across from us. My interactions with Sasha were comfortable and unassuming.

There was no suggestion that our eventful afternoon would be repeated. The only indication it had happened at all was the comfortable way we talked and moved. Before, I had been wound up and tense. I'd jumped at any move from anyone, especially Sasha.

Now, I could smile and joke with everyone. I even laughed a few times.

I'm sure Charlie felt the change immediately. She snorted into her drink when she saw how relaxed Sasha and I were together.

I felt like Sasha and I had established an understanding of one another. We recognized each other. I knew I could go to him should I need anything, but we didn't feel beholden to one another. Rather, we saw that our one afternoon of mutual appreciation cemented the happy memory of embracing life and living in the present.

By cherishing this encounter for the poetry it was, we could continue on our respective journeys.

In times of woe, which always lie ahead, I could pull out the warm memory and draw strength from knowing that someone out there saw me and loved me, however briefly.

After dinner, I caught Charlie on the main deck. I pulled her aside to an area where no one could overhear.

"I see you had quite the lunch," she teased.

I grinned. "It was satisfying. But can you look at something for me? Sasha found it, but I can't get the right angle to see it."

I took off my hat and moved my hair aside, turning my left ear toward her. She stepped closer to examine the tattoo.

"What is that? It looks like a knot-work tattoo, but there's definitely something magical about it."

"Sasha said the port we dock at tomorrow has people like us. Obviously, he saw my ears, but how would he know where the Fae community is?"

She shrugged. "I imagine his search for women to appreciate has taken him to some very interesting places. He's right though. There is a huge Fae community in Rome, and you should get it checked out by a magic expert."

I'm not keen to explore a Fae community, but I guess it's necessary.

"Will you take me there?"

She nodded. "But we can't bring Reilley."

"He already knows I'm Fae."

"Still. He won't be safe."

"He can't wander around alone."

She grinned wickedly. "Why not ask Sasha to go with him?"

"You're joking."

"Do you have a better idea?"

"No," I sighed, defeated.

I left Charlie to search for Sasha. I found him enjoying the evening air at the far end of the main deck.

"Hey, Sasha."

"Good evening, Ember." He turned to me and smiled a very charming smile.

"That mark you noticed earlier, I'm going to get it checked out tomorrow."

"Good." He nodded, satisfied.

"But there is a little problem. Do you think you can help me?"

"What can I do for you?"

"Reilley can't come with me, but he'll still need to buy ingredients for the kitchen. Will you show him around and keep him out of trouble?" I pleaded, knowing this was an unusual request.

"This is not a problem for me, but you should ask him if he wants me as a guide."

"Thank you. I trust you'll keep him safe."

I walked toward the mess hall to break the news to Reilley. In the quarterdeck hallway, I could hear Willie yelling.

"What did I tell you, Runt? Follow the recipes as they're written. Can't you read?"

"But if you add a little salt, it tastes much better." Reilley pleaded his case.

"I took time from my day to write these down for you to make sure you do it right. You aren't even going to use them?"

"It's not that. I just want to make them better."

"I never had this problem with Johnny. As soon as he comes back, you're gone."

"What do you mean?"

"Charlie told me she's bringing him back. Then what are you going to do, Runt?"

"Stop calling me that!" Reilley raised his voice.

There was a loud smack followed by a grunt and a thud. I ran the rest of the way to the mess hall. Willie stood menacingly over Reilley, who was rising to sit. Blood beaded at his mouth.

"Don't you raise your voice at me, Runt," Willie spat.

"What did I say, Willie?" I growled.

Willie's rage made him brave. "What are *you* going to do about it?"

Damn Shy. I knew I'd need my dagger. Getting Reilley out is a higher priority. Plus, I'm not fit enough right now to pull it off.

"I keep my promises. You're not long for this world."

"Empty threats."

"We'll see." I helped Reilley up, putting myself between him and Willie. "Reilley, get your things from your bunk," I said softly.

I waited by the bunk door, staring Willie down. Reilley didn't take long. I motioned for him to go on ahead.

"Enjoy the time you have left. You're a dead man walking," I promised with cold fury. Then I left to take care of Reilley.

Once we were on the main deck, I turned to him and examined his face. His lip was split and bleeding, but that was the worst of his injuries.

"Do you still have that witch hazel?"

He pulled it from his bag and handed it to me. I wet my handkerchief and pressed it to his bleeding lip. He sucked in air, telling me it stung.

"Oh, Reilley," I tsked. "Trouble finds you as often as it does me."

"I don't do it on purpose," he mumbled against the handkerchief.

"I know," I soothed.

"Thank you for helping me, Ember." His tears started to well.

I tried to calm him the way Sasha had calmed me, by running my hand from his shoulder down his arm.

"It's all right," I hushed.

He sniffed hard once. Then he clenched his jaw and didn't let the tears spill.

"I'll get stronger, Ember. I promised I'd protect you. How can I do that like this? I won't cry anymore."

I smiled at him gently. "I used to tell my little brother that tears were a sign of strength because they meant you were facing your fears."

"I didn't know you have a brother. What's his name?"

"Pika."

"You must miss him."

I nodded.

"But you never cry when things get hard, Ember."

"Because I'm not as brave as you," I whispered. "Now, let's get you settled in." I grabbed his bag and ushered him to the deckhand cabin.

"Reilley is staying with us for the night," I announced to Charlie, Mac, and Sasha. "Take Nick's bunk," I told him, smiling inwardly. Then I motioned Mac and Charlie outside.

I told them only that Willie had struck Reilley, and that I removed him from the situation.

"You should talk to Mr. Brewster," Mac suggested.

"I'm headed there now. Keep an eye on him, would you?"

They agreed, and I went to Mr. Brewster's cabin. I knocked at the door and entered when I heard him beckon.

"What can I do for you, Ember?"

I told Brewster what had happened, minus the part about Johnny returning as I hadn't figured that one out yet. I also left out my death threats.

"I'm not here to get Willie in trouble though I think he deserves it. It's not my airship or my decision. I'm here to ask that Reilley be reassigned."

"I think that's a good idea, but we don't have many openings. Do you think he'd accept a position in engineering? It's manual labor."

"I think he'll take anything that gets him away from Willie."

"Fine. I'll notify the foreman. He can start the day shift tomorrow."

"Thank you, Mr. Brewster."

I returned to my bunk, and Reilley was actually excited about starting a new job. Knowing that Reilley was safely within reach, I fell asleep more quickly than usual.

10

Nick was definitely surprised to find Reilley in his bunk the next morning. He flopped down in the dark and caused quite a commotion, which resulted in everyone waking early.

"Come on, Nick. Have a heart. He had nowhere else to sleep," I said innocently.

"You could've at least given me a heads up."

"After the heads up I got yesterday? I wanted it to be a surprise." I grinned.

"Fine. You got me, but I just want to point out, you had help. So you only get half a point."

"Reilley wasn't in on it, so I get two points for getting you both at once."

He screwed up his face thoughtfully. "You really put my generosity to the test. Fine, two points. Hey, Reilley, want to get in on some payback?"

"I'll get back to you," Reilley answered sleepily.

"Good call. Keep her guessing."

The day shift went to breakfast. Willie wore a sour expression as he made breakfast with a borrowed helper. My guess was the hulking man was a temp from engineering. He didn't know his way around a kitchen, but Willie wouldn't be pushing him around.

I guess Brewster will be hiring a new cook in Rome unless Willie was right and Charlie is bringing Johnny back.

I glanced over at Charlie, who ate quietly. She smiled at me when she saw me looking.

We all wished Reilley good luck on his first day in engineering and went about our work. We were due to dock in Rome that night. I was able to put my harness on myself and found my wrist felt a little better. I still had to be careful, but I was able to finish my work before sunset.

After dinner, Reilley chattered excitedly about his day. "I followed the foreman today so he could show me all the jobs in engineering. I learned how electricity turns the gears that wind the springs when we dock. There are even unwound springs in case lightning strikes the ship. That way we get free electricity and the lightning has somewhere safe to go. The springs unwind slowly, which spins the magnets and creates electricity. They power the propeller and rudders that steer the airship. I also saw the big furnace where people shovel minte to make the ship stay up."

"What's minte?" I asked.

"It's a fuel that burns really hot."

"So what job are they going to give you?"

"Right now, they said I need to get stronger, so I'm going to help shovel. But the foreman said Franklin will teach me how to repair the springs and gears, too. So maybe I'll be able to do that in the future."

"That's great, Reilley."

"But, since I work day shift, I can still go into town to have fun when we land this time."

"About that. Charlie and I have something we have to do."

"Okay, I'll go with you."

"I'm sorry. You can't go with us this time."

"Oh." His face fell.

"But Sasha has agreed to show you around so you won't be alone." I tried my best to make that sound fun for him.

"I'd rather stay on the ship," he said seriously.

"Don't you want to see Rome?"

"Not with him."

"Oh come on, it's still Rome. Do you really want to miss it?"

He warred with his desire to see Rome and his determination to dislike Sasha.

"I'll just go alone," he offered.

"Not an option."

He crossed his arms over his chest.

"Reilley, promise me you won't go alone."

He reluctantly agreed.

"Sasha isn't bad. You might even like him. Besides, he's been there many times, so he knows all the fun places."

"Fine. I'll go with *Sasha*," he agreed through pouting lips.

"You'll have fun."

He grunted.

I went to engineering to collect my laundry. By

the time I was washed and changed, we were land-ing. Charlie and I stayed in the cabin until Sasha and Reilley disembarked so we wouldn't blow Charlie's cover to Sasha.

We collected our pay at the dock and continued down the hill the ship had docked on. The city was lively after dark. Lamps shined off marble and sparkling fountains. Charlie walked with determina-tion through the narrow streets, and I followed close behind.

The street cafés were crowded, and patrons drank wine and toasted each other. The food smells made my mouth water. The dark-featured locals ate, drank, sang, and argued with grand gestures and loud voices. We easily slipped through the rambunc-tious crowds unnoticed.

We passed a huge amphitheater, crumbling with age. Finally, I followed Charlie into a little café. Customers sat at small tables drinking warm liquid from tiny cups. We went through a door at the back of the café, which led us downstairs to a basement where an elderly woman ground potent smelling beans.

"Ciao, Nonna," Charlie said and dropped her glamour.

"Ciao, bambina," the old woman responded and indicated toward a nearby rug.

Charlie threw back the rug to reveal a trap door and opened it. She climbed down a ladder and motioned up at me to follow. My landing echoed on the surrounding stone of the torch-lit tunnel.

I trailed Charlie through a series of narrow passageways. We turned another corner, and the tunnel opened wide enough for merchant stalls and the Fae foot-traffic that frequented them.

I turned to Charlie in shock, and she watched me with untamed eyes.

"This many?" I asked.

"You aren't the only exile. Your stepmother has uprooted many."

I pulled my hat lower to hide more of my face.

"Is there anything you need to buy?"

"I need a new dagger."

"Look around a bit. I'm going to ask after a magic expert."

I nodded to her and started to browse the shop stalls. I found a stall that sold weapons and started searching for a dagger to replace the one Shy took. I picked up one of the right size and examined it. Feeling its heft and balance, I inspected the blade. Etched into the blade near the hilt was a bird drinking from a teacup.

"Human made," the stall owner informed me as I admired the dagger. "Far superior to anything you'd find in Faerie."

"Why is that?" I asked.

"It's made of steel, so it burns when it cuts Fae. Also, it was made by Tea Jay Inc., so it comes with all the best functionality."

"And what functionality does this dagger have, besides being sharp?"

He held out his hand, and I gave it to him.

"This is called the Quill. Watch carefully."

He pointed to two jewels on one side of the hilt. He used his thumb to shift one of the jewels toward the pommel. Then he pointed the blade at a piece of wood hung on the stone wall behind him. Pressing the other jewel, the blade shot out of the hilt and stuck in the wood.

"Impressive."

"The blade can be put back, should it be retrievable."

I purchased it with human coins immediately. It even fit in my boot sheath. *I call that a win.*

Charlie found me just as I was contemplating a tray of fresh honey buns.

"I think I found someone who can help." She beckoned me to follow.

We navigated the twisting tunnels into a quiet residential area. The passages were narrower, and doorways to homes were gouged into the rock.

Charlie knocked on an unassuming, wooden door, which didn't fit its opening. A cough bid us enter into a small, one-room living space. Sitting at a table was a man I knew well.

"Eamonn?"

"Little princess, is that you?" he whispered with wonder.

"It's not a good time to address me like that, Eamonn. Why're you here?"

"Your stepmother does not think me qualified to teach magic to your brother, or anyone for that matter. After she dismissed me, no one wanted me. I came here to teach the outcast children."

"But you're the best teacher in all of Faerie!"

"It seems the queen would disagree, but no matter. My dear, you look very well. I'm glad to know you're safe. There are many others who'd also rejoice in this knowledge."

"Please don't tell anyone you've seen me, Eamonn. That would put us both in danger."

"But of course you're right. It shall be my joy alone. What brings you here?"

"We found a mark that defies explanation."

"Show me."

I removed my hat and pulled my hair aside, turning my ear toward him.

"Have you been able to use magic since you left Faerie?"

"Not even a glamour. She stripped my magic."

"Not stripped, bound. She bound your magic with this seal."

"Can you break it?"

"Yes, but it may be exhausting for you. How's your health?"

I explained about my wrist and bruised side.

"I'll heal those first. How long do we have?"

I turned to Charlie. "We leave tomorrow after lunch," she answered.

"Not much time then. We must start immediately."

As he puttered around for the materials he needed to heal my injuries and break the seal, he reminisced.

"Sprained wrist? Bruised side? It reminds me of when you and Liam used to fight."

"We weren't fighting, Eamonn. We were training."

"And that's just what you said then, coming to me with all manner of injuries that you wanted to hide from your father."

"He only let me train if I didn't get hurt. Besides, Liam was injured more than I."

"Oh aye, but he still grew into a strong lad. Captain of the royal guard is he now?"

I nodded bitterly. *I still can't believe Liam accepted the assignment to ensure I went through the portal.* "Prove your loyalty," *Helena had said.*

I clenched my teeth when I thought about how I'd begged him to come with me.

Eamonn reached for my wrist, and I handed it into his familiar hands.

"I remember when your father first brought you to Faerie. Your uncle was still king, mourning the death of his wife as your father mourned your mother. 'Be strong, little cub,' he would tell you, and you'd make such a fierce little face. He brought you to me as a distraction. He wasn't even sure you had magic. But you inherited all of your father's magic, except his fire. We watched you so closely when you came of age to see if the fire would show. By then, your father had remarried, and your brother was already ten. You were so much different than the girl we all knew. Pika was the only one you would smile for. Your father and I didn't know what to do."

Apathy was my only safety from Helena. She destroyed so many people I loved.

"All right. Are you ready to break the seal?"

I nodded.

"Lie back and turn the mark toward me."

I lay on his bed and tilted my head as directed.

"You'll feel an inner tugging, and the seal will fight back. Try to push your magic through as I pull the seal."

Exhausting was an understatement. I attempted every spell I'd ever learned. Nothing seemed to work. Finally, I tried a memory spell. I called forth the memory closest to the surface, my arrival in Faerie.

Warm sunlight kissed my skin. My father had told me many things along the journey here. He explained who he was, what I was, and what had happened to my mother. My heart mourned her loss, but he assured me we'd meet again.

My new home was enchanting. Gleaming white rocks covered with moss and ivy made the walls glint in the sun. We passed through archways held aloft with columns. We approached a large, metal gate, and my father knocked on a small, wooden door to one side.

A boy around my age opened it. He looked up at my father and then turned his untamed eyes on me. Golden curls encircled his curious face.

"Liam, don't just answer the door without knowing who it is." A man stepped up behind the boy.

"Rick!" the man exclaimed and embraced my father. "We've been worried."

"I know. I'm sorry," my father said, kneeling beside me. "Ember, this is my dear old friend, Lee, and his son, Liam. Why don't you and Liam go play while I talk to Lee?"

I clung to my father.

"Be strong, little cub. I'm sure Liam knows fun games. Don't you, Liam?"

"I know all the best games," Liam pronounced proudly. He held out his hand to me. His warm smile and golden curls endeared this boy with the untamed eyes to me. I took his hand without hesitation.

Back in Eamonn's bed, I lay limp in a pool of my own sweat. Opening my eyes, I saw Eamonn smile down at me. The dimly-lit room seemed too bright. The haze, which I'd gotten used to after my magic was bound, had cleared. Everything felt too sharp and overwhelming.

"There she is. Where did you go? Someplace nice, I hope."

"Is it broken?" I croaked, dropping the memory like it had burned me.

"Indeed, it is." He smiled triumphantly. "But I should warn you, the caster of the spell will feel that it's gone."

Shit. You could've told me that before.

"We have to leave. We're cutting it close," Charlie said, her brows knit with worry.

I sat up, and the room spun. Eamonn caught and steadied me.

"Easy," he instructed. "My dear, could we have a moment?" he asked Charlie.

"Of course." She closed the door as she stepped outside.

He walked to his cabinet and pulled out a seashell. "Take this with you."

"I can't take that." I stared at him in horror. "It's too valuable."

"Ember, listen to me. Rough times lie ahead for you. I can feel it. You know the spell. Use it to contact me should you need me."

I took the shell reluctantly and placed is carefully in my pack.

"Now go. May your feet be swift and soundless on the journey ahead."

"We'll meet again," I promised as I left.

11

We left the tunnels as quickly as we could, taking the first exit we found. As we departed from an inconspicuous garden door, it took Charlie a few moments to figure out the right way back to the airship.

The sun shone bright overhead as we raced through the streets and climbed the hill where the ship was moored. The rest of the deckhands were just loading the last boxes into cargo.

"Cutting it a little close, aren't we?" Mac censured.

Charlie and I apologized as we tried to catch our breaths.

"Just glad you made it."

We passed through the quarterdeck from the cargo hold. I saw Reilley shoveling minte in engineering as we walked to the main deck. He wore a sleeveless shirt, and his pale skin glistened with sweat and smudged soot. I didn't distract him but went to the main deck equipment room to gear up.

The daylight was half over, and I needed to get to work.

"Are you all right to work? Not too tired?" Charlie asked me.

"No problem. I'm a little tired, but that memory spell knocked me out for a while."

"All right, see you at dinner." She grabbed her equipment.

"Hey," I stopped her from leaving. "Thanks."

She smiled and rushed to work. I put my bag by my bunk, then I did the same.

I could work at my normal pace since my wrist and side were healed. I wasn't quick enough to finish before dinner though. I climbed down when the bell rang and set a goal to try to use every bit of daylight after dinner.

I cast a glamour over my ears after putting my equipment away. Reilley waited impatiently for me at the bottom of the stairs leading from the main deck to engineering.

"Ember, where have you been? Did you take care of whatever it was?"

"Yes, it's taken care of. So did you have fun? What did you and Sasha do?" I asked as we made our way to the mess hall.

"Sasha told me he wanted to show me the beauty and grace of the female form. I was a little nervous at first, but he was right."

I stared at him in shock. As he kept talking, my horror grew.

"It was embarrassing to see that much skin, but Sasha said it was to see her better. She was so flexible and graceful, too."

I started to feel angry at Sasha for whatever he'd gotten Reilley into.

"And she was so sparkly," he finished, staring into the distance.

"Wait. What? Sparkly?" *I think I got lost.* "Where exactly did Sasha take you?"

He stared at me, amazed, like it was obvious. "He took me to a little theater to see the belly dancers."

I blinked, my mind blank. Then I sighed. *I need to talk to Reilley about storytelling and which pieces need to come first.*

"Ah, belly dancers. That does sound fun. They are talented, aren't they?" I smoothed over like I'd known the whole time.

He beamed and nodded with enthusiasm.

After arriving in the mess hall, we grabbed plates of food. The new cook was inconspicuously average. He wasn't too big or small, dark or light. He was the kind of person who goes unnoticed.

I sat next to Sasha, and I was surprised when Reilley sat on his other side.

"Belly dancers?" I whispered so only Sasha could hear.

He shrugged. "Now, he can look at a woman and see beauty and grace instead of being afraid."

I thought about that for a while.

Even though Reilley was unconscious and can't remember, he still knows his last sexual encounter, and likely his first, was with a female predator. The bodies of their partners often intimidate first timers. Predators can ruin a person's sexual health. Seeing a scantily-clad woman move in an alluring way in a non-threatening environment may help him feel more comfortable in future sexual encounters.

I looked over at Reilley, who ate happily. *Clearly, he enjoyed the experience.*

My eyes shifted back to Sasha, who smiled charmingly before taking a drink. *I guess Sasha made a good call.* I gave Sasha a winning smile as a reward. I couldn't remember the last time I'd let a full smile break.

His answering expression was full of heat. Before I could decide how to respond, Reilley dropped his fork, which clanged as it hit his plate. He blushed hard and lowered his face. I stared at the appealing expression, but my steady gaze seemed to increase his embarrassment.

He rose from the table. "I have a little more work to do," he explained in a rush. Then he left.

Looking back at Sasha, the flame of desire had been snubbed out. He just stared back curiously.

"Actually, I want to get more work done, also," I said, shoveling down my last few bites.

I didn't finish completely before twilight, but I did get a lot more done. Climbing down to the main deck, I removed my equipment, washed, and changed clothes. Then I took a walk to let my hair dry.

I let my mind wander, and it landed on Liam. A pang made my stomach turn. *I haven't felt like this since I was sixteen, before I became numb.*

A gust of wind blew the hair back from my face, and I stared over the railing into the inky night.

I held my breath as I waited in the abandoned courtyard, listening hard for soft footsteps on the stone paths. Though I couldn't see them in the dark of night, I knew that weeds and wildflowers grew untamed, encroaching the stone walkways to and from this hushed haven. So many times we had met here to escape the chains of home. We played, trained, laughed, and sang in this deserted place where no one else came.

What started as the inseparability of childish attachment grew into a flame of love and passion. Tonight, that fiery urge would finally be consummated. My breath sounded loud in my ears as I tried to breathe softly. My skin felt cold compared to the heat I knew his touch would bring.

The scuffle of boots on stone announced his approach. I cast a Fae light in the lantern on the ground beside me. He stepped into its glow. Its soft light played in his golden curls and glittered in his untamed eyes.

"Liam," I whispered like a prayer. I rushed to his arms, but, for the first time, he held me off.

I looked up into his face. He wore a cold, unfeeling expression.

"Liam, what is it? Are you all right?"

"I can't." He sounded dead.

"What do you mean?" My voice shook with the rest of my body.

"It's over."

I stepped back in shock. "Liam, I don't understand. What happened?" The fear that Liam always kept at bay started to creep in. "Did she get to you?" I whispered.

"This isn't about her. This is about you and me. I just don't love you like that."

I tried to grasp the situation and work through the pit that was my gut.

"Did she threaten you? Did she threaten me? Liam, you know she just wants to see me suffer. That's why she's trying to turn you away from me. But I can endure it if you're with me. We can overcome anything together. We can run away and hide. I'll leave my father and brother just to be with you."

"You don't get it!" He raised his voice. "I don't want to be with you. All that stuff I said before was a lie. We should've just stayed friends, but now even that's ruined. We'll see each other at the palace, but I won't meet you here again."

He turned to leave, but I grabbed his hand.

"I don't believe you," I said with confidence. "Kiss me one more time and prove to me you don't love me."

He sighed but knew the determination in my voice. This was the only way I'd let go. He stepped close and put one hand on my lower back. The other cupped my face as he dipped his head toward me.

"Ember," he mouthed before our lips met.

I knew the bittersweet kiss would be our last. I knew he loved me but was still leaving me alone. Tears streamed down my face as I savored our goodbye.

He broke from our final kiss and strode into the night, not looking back. I stood alone in the faint glow of a single Fae light, tears flowing as my heart broke for the last time.

On the main deck, I felt the heartbreak that had switched on the apathy and frozen my insides. The wind blew my dry hair from my face and froze the tear tracks to my cheeks.

I fought the encroaching chill that threatened to freeze my newly melted ice, rubbing at the frozen tears as someone approached.

Indulal meandered toward me and stopped to bid me good evening. He smiled compassionately and waited in companionable silence.

"Thank you," I said finally. "You were right. The pain is far better than drifting in the cold."

He tilted his head and bowed to me gracefully as if to say, "at your service."

"Tell me, Indulal. How have you become so wise? How did you know what I needed?"

He silently collected his thoughts for a moment. "Wisdom is relative. I know the greatest wisdom is acknowledging I still have much to learn. I recognized the apathy you were hiding in because I too have escaped into it."

"What happened?" I whispered before decorum could stop me.

He paused, then continued softly while staring out into the night, his dark eyes reflecting the deep vastness of the clear sky. "In my homeland, I loved a woman in a position far above mine. I had not even a hope of a chance. By some miracle, she returned my love. We were secretly married, and she soon conceived my child. We made plans to flee, but a man above her status decided he would possess her. When she refused, he took her against her will. He discovered she was not as untouched as he wanted her. He murdered her and paid her family for their loss. I tried to avenge her, but he was unreachable. That is when apathy came for me. I wandered for many years before stumbling upon a temple, where the monks nursed me back to health physically and mentally."

I stared at Indulal, not knowing how to respond.

"What was her name?"

"Chandra."

"I'm sorry she and your child were taken from you. I hope you will see them again someday."

"I know I will," he said faithfully.

We shared a silence amid the feeling of longing for those who waited for us.

I gazed out into the dark.

"It is always darker when there is water rather than land below," he observed.

"Are we over water?" I squinted toward the ground.

"The Norwegian Sea."

Searching the darkness, I squinted at a light waving in the distance.

"What's that?" I pointed.

"It looks...like a signal torch," he said hesitantly while wrinkling his brow.

A soft whistling preceded the splintering of wood as something suddenly stuck into the hull below where we stood. I peered over the side at a large, metal arrow with a thick, metal cord attached.

"Ring the bell!" Indulal yelled. The bell's harsh clang pierced the otherwise silent night.

My heart vibrated as though the bell's clapper was striking it directly, but I took a steadying breath before pulling my boot-dagger from its sheath and tensing for a fight.

"Hold them off," Indulal told me. He ran to the equipment shed, where Mac and Sasha emerged carrying heavy, iron tools.

My skin hummed with anticipation while I scanned the deck and railing near me. On my left, not three feet away, a hand with thick, calloused fingers grabbed the railing from the outside. Its match crept up alongside it before their combined strength hefted their owner onto the deck. His thin lips turned up in a malicious grin, causing his weathered face to crease.

With a well-trained lunge and no hesitation, I swiftly slashed his throat in the time it took me to steadily exhale. His dark eyes widened as he gurgled his last breath and tumbled backward toward the sea.

The rumbling of many hurried footsteps announced the reinforcements from engineering as they poured from the stairwell. Armed with everything from fire stokers to devices that shot small projectiles, their soot-smeared faces tensed with the same anticipation as the rest of us.

As we crowded the deck with our backs toward each other, our hush was shattered with a deafening bang as an engineer's weapon shot a projectile into the chest of an attacker. I didn't have time to voice my surprise when his chest leaked blood and he collapsed because his comrades arrived in force.

Chaos erupted on the main deck as countless pirates boarded our ship. The shouts and grunts as people fought for their lives, the crack of shots fired, the clash of blades, and the steady clang of the alarm bell all mixed together into a far off muffle until the only sounds I heard properly were those of my deep breaths and the strong beating of my heart.

My second opponent proved more agile than my first. He dodged the swipe of my dagger a few times before Charlie struck him down from behind with a large hammer; his skull cracked audibly before he collapsed in a heap. Charlie and I exchanged a quick nod before separating to continue our fights.

After I crossed blades with a pirate who never seemed to aim at my vital spots, I took a chance to look around at the other confrontations. I noted that in multiple melees, the invaders had opted to incapacitate, restrain, or injure our crew rather than pursue easy kills.

Reilley's voice intruded upon my observations and the distant hum of battle. "Ember, duck!"

I evaded a blow to the head from behind and heard the crack from Reilley's weapon. The projectile crackled like static as it flew over me and struck my attacker. I squinted, my mouth agape, as his teeth chattered and he convulsed, went rigid, and toppled to the deck.

"Thanks," I said breathlessly to Reilley.

I scanned him anxiously for injuries as his frantic eyes traveled swiftly over my face and body. A black smudge streaked across his cheek, but he seemed unharmed. We both let out a sigh of relief. A quick glance around showed our crewmen were losing. Many lay strewn across the deck, unconscious or injured. I felt a rush of pride to see that Charlie still swung her hammer, keeping an adversary at bay.

Finally, a man stepped onto our deck, his movements confident and self-important.

"Stand down," he ordered. The pirates immediately stopped attacking.

Our captain stepped out of the fray. "What is the meaning of this?" she demanded.

"Surrender your goods, or we'll blow your ship from the air." The pirate captain presented his terms.

Our captain glared at the pirate, her eyes filled with determined fire. "Fine, but leave my people unharmed."

"Some of my men have been injured or killed. Your deckhands will help transport the goods to our ship. Agree to this, and no further injury will come to you or your crew."

Our captain nodded. "Deckhands!" she called.

Mac, Indulal, Sasha, Charlie, and I came forward. Nick lay unconscious and sprawled on the deck, so Reilley stepped up to take his place.

"Move the cargo onto their ship quickly and return safely," she ordered.

At the pirate captain's command, some of the pirates remained on the main deck to keep our crew from revolting. The rest descended to cargo with us.

We opened the hull and ran a gangplank from our ship to theirs, carefully carrying our goods to their cargo hold. The ocean churned black far below the unsteady gangplank as if mimicking the turmoil in my gut.

Making quick work of the transfer, we dropped the last boxes in their hold and started for our ship. Indulal crossed first, and Charlie stepped up to follow him. As she put her foot onto the gangplank, the pirate ship lurched to the side, and the plank shuddered and plummeted toward the sea. Charlie fell back against us as we crowded the exit.

With the type of desperation only the abandoned know, Charlie, Mac, Sasha, Reilley, and I watched our ship float away.

Before anyone could gasp or protest, the hum of quickly turning gears whirled through the hull. I flinched as a boom from above rattled the cargo hold. While widening my stance to maintain balance in the aftershock, the hair on my neck and arms stood up as a zing of electricity traveled along the metal cable from the pirate ship to our vessel's hull.

The bolt sparked a flame, which slowly began to consume our airship. More metal arrows shot from the pirate ship, piercing the envelope.

Charlie's wail echoed the one in my heart as the five of us—the only survivors—witnessed our ship and its crew plummet toward the ocean in flames.

12

The pirate captain, accompanied by our newly-hired cook, approached from the other end of the cargo hold.

"So," the pirate captain started, "which one of you is Ember?"

"You said no harm would come to them," I growled.

"Wrong. I said they would not be injured. They aren't injured. They're dead. Your captain should've chosen her terms more carefully. Now, are you Ember?" He looked to our cook, who nodded helpfully.

"What do you want with me?" I demanded.

"What we want is the bounty for delivering you to your stepmother's agent."

A chill spread through me from my gut.

"Will you be a good prisoner and come quietly?"

"Not on your life."

"I never would've guessed you'd say that," he said with mock surprise. "Simmons."

"Aye, Sir," our cook responded.

"Put them all in the brig."

The pirates escorted us to a metal cage with weapons at our backs. They shoved us in and locked the door. Simmons smiled as he pocketed the key.

"Don't worry. We'll arrive shortly," Simmons promised.

They left us to stew, and my mind scrambled to find an escape. The sturdy metal bars of the cage weren't going anywhere. Looking through the bars, I saw the walls of the hold were the curved wood that made up the hull. Cargo and provisions took up the bulk of the dark space. A lamp near us dimly illuminated the inside of the cage, so we could make out each other's faces.

Silent tears streaked down Reilley's cheeks, and he shook with emotion. He didn't make a sound as he tried to pull himself together. Charlie was white with the numbness that follows a shock. Sasha and Mac were withdrawn and mourned internally. I didn't have time to feel at the moment. I had to figure out how to get us to safety. First, I removed my boot-dagger and sheath from my boot and nestled them between my breasts in case the pirates decided to search us for weapons.

"At least we're alive," Mac commented as he sat in the corner of the cell.

"What are we going to do, Ember?" Reilley looked to me for guidance.

"Let me think," I instructed.

"Ember, I have something to tell you," Charlie confessed softly.

"Can it wait?"

She shook her head. "Remember when I told you my brother killed my lover?"

I nodded and wondered where this was going.

"That was a lie. My brother didn't kill Johnny. My brother snatched him at your stepmother's behest. They ordered me to spy on you and tell them where our next ports were. Otherwise, they would torture and kill him." She sobbed for her lover and the betrayal she'd committed.

"Johnny?"

She nodded. "The cook before Reilley."

A bitter taste invaded my mouth. *I knew trust was a mistake.* Betrayal was a flavor I knew well, but it wasn't going to distract me.

"I understand," I said coldly. Charlie moved close to Mac and buried her head in his chest, crying silently.

Reilley stepped close to me, and I turned my cold stare on him. *Did you betray me too, Reilley?*

He placed a firm hand on my shoulder and looked at me with compassion. "What can I do to help?" he offered.

"Just stay out of my way," I spat.

He flinched, then nodded sadly before he sat in another corner and watched me pace the cell.

Sasha interrupted my concentration. "They have told us what they plan for you, Ember, but what of the rest of us?"

"That's a good question." Simmons walked into the lamplight. "The captain would like to extend an invitation to you and the ginger to join our crew."

"What about Charlie and Reilley?" Mac asked.

"There's no room for them. They'll be sold as sex

slaves as soon as we inspect their quality." Simmons smiled, and his eyes twinkled at the prospect.

Reilley and Charlie paled to hear their fates, and I ground my teeth in fury.

"I am afraid I have to decline," Sasha said courteously.

"I'd rather die," Mac growled.

"What a shame," Simmons lamented. "Oh well, we're in much need of entertainment. Your deaths will not go to waste."

Simmons pulled a mask over his nose and mouth. Then he produced a can like the spray I used to fix the envelope. After he sprayed it into our cell, a salty odor stung my nose and throat.

When I awoke on the floor, I sat up and looked around the cell. Reilley and Charlie slumped against the bars, unconscious. Sasha and Mac were gone. The only indication of their whereabouts was the rowdy shouts and jeers from the pirate crew above deck.

I crawled to Reilley and shook him awake.

"What's going on?" he mumbled.

"I don't know, but it's not good."

After Reilley was awake enough to be afraid, he woke Charlie as well. Huddling together, we planned our escape.

After a while, the shouts became quiet, and the ship started to descend.

Simmons approached the cage. Since it was only him, I was convinced he'd take me first, which worked right into our plan. I stepped forward, ready to grab the dagger they didn't know I had as soon as I had maneuvering room.

"Not you." Simmons pushed me farther into the cell. "Him." He pointed at Reilley.

I looked at Reilley as our plan disintegrated. He wore a determined expression, which worried me. He lunged for Simmons' weapon aimed at his chest. A shot echoed through the hull, and Reilley crumbled to the floor; blood seeped into his shirt.

A burning fury built in my gut as I watched Reilley bleed. I turned my attention to Simmons, who stood over him.

One word came to me, and I said it with purpose. "Ignite."

My voice echoed as fire leapt at my demand and swallowed Simmons in blue flames. He was reduced to ash before he could scream.

I rushed to Reilley, my only concern. I pushed up his shirt and discovered a hole in his side where the projectile had punctured him.

"Reilley? Can you hear me?" I called.

His face was contorted with pain, but his emerald eyes met mine as I knelt beside him.

"Ember, are you okay?" he gasped.

"You idiot. Charlie, do you know any healing spells?"

"I should be able to stop the bleeding, but I can't heal the injury entirely." She leaned over him to cast her spell.

Footsteps sounded on the stairs as pirates responded to the sound of Simmons' weapon. I dispatched the scouts quickly and quietly with my dagger.

"All right," Charlie said, helping Reilley to sit. He winced but looked stable enough.

We each supported an arm as we moved as quickly as he could toward the cargo hull door. Charlie opened it, and we looked out. The ground was twenty feet below, and the ship was still descending.

Charlie and I chanted a hover charm together and hoped for the best as we stepped from the hull. We raced toward the ground. Wind thumped in my ears, and my stomach lurched as we fell. Two feet before crashing, the charm took effect and halted our impact.

Touching the ground gently, we tried to run, but Reilley couldn't make it. We managed to take cover in a group of trees.

The airship was docking, and the pirates would come looking for us. Charlie and I made eye contact over Reilley, who lay in the grass.

"I'm sorry. I hope one day you can forgive me, and we can truly be friends," Charlie said sincerely. Then she changed her glamour to look like me and ran from the trees toward the pirate ship.

She caught the pirates' attention and ran in the opposite direction of where Reilley and I were hiding. The pirates, fooled by her glamour, gave chase.

"Reilley," I whispered, leaning in close to him. "Can you move?"

Reilley's eyes, clouded with pain, found mine. "Ember, they're after you. You'll be faster without me." He pleaded for me to leave him.

"Not a chance." I helped him to his feet.

We hobbled for a long time through the forest before we came upon a small spring. I helped Reilley sit, propped against a tree. I approached the clear, cool water and cupped a handful.

Let this water purify and fortify Reilley. Help me heal him.

I brought the handful of water to him, and he drank. I repeated this a few times until his thirst was quenched. He looked a little stronger as we rested by the forest spring. He fell asleep, and I didn't wake him.

I need to find Reilley a healer. I wish I had that seashell Eamonn gave me. I could really use his help right now.

Too tired to think properly, I sat next to Reilley and let his blond head rest on my shoulder. I fell asleep trying to work out what we should do next.

Pika and I waved goodbye to our father as he rode through the palace gates.

"Why do you think Papa is going to Water Clan territory?" Pika asked.

"I don't know. He said he had important business to discuss, but he wouldn't give me any details."

I looked over at him, surprised by his serious expression. *He's growing up fast.* I wrapped my arm around his shoulders. He was almost as tall as me.

"Let's do something fun, eh?" I smiled at him.

"I wish I could, but Mother wants me to study more this afternoon. Will you meet me later at the frog pond?"

I nodded, and he squeezed my hand before leaving me alone. As Pika walked away, the cold crept back into me. I readjusted to its comforting chill and decided some training wouldn't be a bad idea.

Heading to the practice range where the guards trained, I was surprised to see it was deserted. In the armory, I grabbed a handful of daggers and returned to the range. Since there was no one to spar with, I settled for throwing the daggers at targets.

The exercise was relaxing, and I soon found a rhythm. As I went to retrieve the daggers from the target, the sound of a solid stride caught my attention. I turned toward whomever had entered the range.

Golden curls shined in the afternoon sun as Liam stopped short at seeing me.

"Liam," I greeted him indifferently.

"Princess." He nodded coldly as usual.

"Ember," a tall guard-in-training called from behind Liam, waving at me cheerfully.

"Duncan." I smiled at him as he came toward me.

"I looked for you earlier. Why didn't you come at the usual time? I had to spar with someone else." Duncan pouted.

"My father was leaving, so I went to see him off."

Liam went about preparing for training and ignored our presence.

Duncan looked around at him to make sure he couldn't hear. Then he stepped close to me familiarly and whispered in a husky voice, "Can I come to you tonight?"

"I told you our time was up, Duncan. I don't want you to get hurt."

"Oh come on, who's going to hurt me? Are you sure this whole 'for a season' thing isn't just you being afraid that you'll really like me?"

I sighed at his naivety. *It's too dangerous. What if she thinks I really care about him?* I bit my lip nervously and looked back at him. *He's cute, but I'm in no danger of falling for him. Still...*

Duncan smiled an alluring grin and reached up to tuck a strand of hair behind my ear. "It's been awhile. Haven't you missed me a little?"

It has been awhile, too long. The coil inside me tightened as I felt his arousal. *One more time shouldn't hurt, right? I mean, I haven't shown him any particular favor.* "All right," I agreed. "Meet me in the usual place."

His smile broadened with excitement, and he strutted away to go about his training. As I left the range, I looked over at Liam to ensure he hadn't heard the exchange. He drew back his bow with a clenched jaw, not paying any attention. I left the range looking forward to my tryst later that night.

The summer heat cooled down only slightly when the sun went down. I left my room quietly as the moon rose above the trees. I didn't need any light as I followed the familiar path to our rendezvous point. Eventually, the stone path gave way to dirt with overgrown weeds, and I knew the walls around the palace grounds crumbled with age. I found the collapsed wall without fail and leapt over its waist-height remains.

"Duncan," I whispered into the night, squinting to look for him.

He didn't answer.

I whistled softly and called to him again.

He still didn't respond.

Reaching the willow, I spread the curtain of branches to enter our usual meeting spot. Duncan stood, leaning against the tree.

"There you are. Why didn't you answer?"

His silence was uncharacteristic and unnerving.

"Duncan...?" I asked, unsure.

When he didn't reply, my heart skipped a beat. I cast a Fae light to see who exactly was there in Duncan's place. I gasped as the glow of the Fae light floated from my hand toward Duncan's slumped form. An arrow through the chest held him up, and there was a gaping hole where his heart had been.

Oh, Duncan. I'm sorry. I stared at his mutilated corpse with pity, but I didn't shed any tears. I sighed and started back to the palace to bring a guard to help me carry him back and lay him to rest.

After a long night of taking care of Duncan, I finally returned to my room. I washed away the dirt and blood, then moved toward my bed to fall into an exhausted sleep. On the bedside table was an ornate chest with a creamy envelope propped up against it. I picked it up and broke the seal. Helena's elegant script scrawled over the thick parchment.

The only gift any woman truly desires is the heart of someone she holds dear. —H

A shock of guilt churned in my icy stomach as I reached for the chest. Opening it, the bloody image of Duncan's heart seared into my brain, and I snapped the lid shut.

A twig cracked underfoot, announcing a visitor and jarring me awake. Twilight had descended on the forest. Listening hard, I heard soft footsteps coming toward us. I unsheathed my dagger and crouched into a fighting stance.

Stepping from nearby bushes, a man froze when he saw a dagger pointed in his direction. His chestnut hair played around his pointed ears, and his untamed eyes announced that he was Fae.

"Easy," he hushed and raised his hand in a calming gesture.

"What do you want?" I demanded.

"We were just passing through, and I came to find fresh water."

"Who's we?"

"A group of refugees. We travel around to make a living. Our campsite isn't far from here."

I squinted at him to discern his trustworthiness. Then I looked over my shoulder at Reilley. "Do you have a healer? My friend is injured."

He looked behind me at Reilley, and I tensed. "We do. If you put away your dagger, I'll show you the way."

I sheathed my dagger and moved to Reilley's side. "Reilley," I whispered to wake him.

His eyes fluttered open.

"We're going to get you help."

He grunted as I helped him to his feet. The Fae man moved to assist, but my icy glare stopped him from coming near. He held up his hands in surrender and backed off. He filled two buckets with spring water and told us to follow him.

We trudged through the forest as quickly as Reilley could. Finally, we came upon a clearing. Fae, and a few humans, made camp from a couple of wagons. Some stopped and watched our approach.

"Meleana," the man addressed a human woman with short, dark hair. "Please, fetch Nadya. Someone is injured."

The woman rushed to one of the tents pitched in the clearing.

When Meleana returned, an elderly Fae woman accompanied her. She glanced at me, and then her attention went to Reilley. She reached toward him, and I tensed.

"May I help your friend?" Nadya addressed me.

I nodded.

She approached Reilley and asked me what had happened. I told her about the projectile and what Charlie had done to help. She nodded and instructed me to help him into her tent.

I lay him down on a cot, and she knelt beside him. I knelt at his other side and held his hand. He looked up at me.

"It's all right, Reilley. Nadya is a healer. She's going to help you."

He spared a look in Nadya's direction, and she smiled at him encouragingly. Then his eyes locked on mine. Every moment that passed with his steady gaze on me, I willed him to heal.

"Your friend did a good job of stopping the bleeding," I heard Nadya say.

She opened Reilley's shirt and began to work. Whenever he winced, he tried to turn his head to watch her. I put my free hand on his cheek and kept his eyes on mine. This calmed his anxiety considerably.

When Nadya had finished, she addressed me. "He needs sleep now. He'll heal much faster. When was the last time you ate?"

"I don't know," I replied.

She nodded toward the Fae man who'd found us. "Andrei will get you some food."

I looked back at Reilley. "Reilley, go to sleep for a while. I won't be far away. I'll come back after I eat, all right?"

"Okay," he whispered and closed his heavy lids.

I followed Andrei from the tent. He walked toward a fire where stew bubbled in a large pot. He ladled some into a bowl and handed it to me.

We sat near the fire. "Thank you for helping us." I dipped my head at Andrei.

He nodded his acknowledgment. A thick silence descended between us.

"What is your name?"

"Emerald, but you can call me Em," I lied smoothly, not sure if I could trust him.

"Nadya's a wonderful healer. Your lover will be returned to you just fine, Em."

I choked on a bit of potato. "Reilley isn't my lover," I corrected. Sasha's smiling face swam before my eyes. I grew quiet and stared into the stew.

"Eat," Andrei urged.

I looked up at him. His expression had changed. His interest made itself known. *But what kind of interest?* His untamed eyes were shadowed with mystery. As he met my eyes across the fire, intrigue beckoned me to discover this man, like a misty shadow pulling me forward.

"You can come to me should you need anything. Goodnight, Em." He left me to finish my stew.

I ate thoughtfully and returned to Nadya's tent. Reilley slept soundly in the cot. I grabbed a blanket and lay on the ground next to him.

I was relieved we were safe though so many others didn't make it. The faces of those lost didn't let me sleep for some time. I slept soundly once a misty shadow wrapped my mind in its cool caress.

13

I awoke the next morning with the feeling I was being watched. Opening my eyes, I saw Reilley, lying on his side, with his green eyes fixed on my face.

"Good morning, Ember," he said seriously.

"How're you feeling?" I asked, sitting.

He sat as well. "I feel stiff, but not at all like I was shot."

I looked at him sternly. "Why would you rush that pirate? You were almost killed."

I expected him to flinch or look sheepish. Instead, he stared at me, all seriousness. "I promised I'd protect you, and you made it out unharmed. I will not apologize for keeping my word."

Whoa. My mouth fell open at Reilley's response.

"Thank you for protecting me, Reilley, but please don't put yourself in danger again."

He smiled at me softly. "I'm sorry I worried you though."

I looked up at the gentle Reilley I was used to.

"And thank you for rescuing me." His emerald eyes peeked up through a thick curtain of lashes.

A tapping on the flap of the tent announced a visitor.

"Call me Em while we're around them," I whispered to Reilley in a rush.

He nodded without asking questions.

Nadya entered a moment later.

"How are you feeling?" she asked Reilley.

"I'm well thanks to you."

"My pleasure." She smiled.

"Nadya, Andrei said you travel to make a living. What is it you do?" I asked.

"We're entertainers."

"How can we repay you for your kindness to us?"

"Repayment is not necessary. However, I'd like to invite you both to join our band."

I need to get to Eamonn to address the discovery of my fire.

"Where are you headed?"

"Oh, we wander all over."

"Are you going through Rome?"

"We usually make our way through Rome, yes."

I turned to Reilley. "I have a friend there I need to see. Do you mind traveling with them, Reilley?"

"Of course not," he replied.

"Excellent. Now, what entertaining talents do you have?" Nadya inquired.

"What kind of talents are you looking for? I can fight, throw knives, and dance," I said.

"I can cook and play the hand drum," Reilley offered.

Nadya thought for a moment, then smiled. "Let's see what you can do."

Reilley and I followed her out of the tent. The small group of Fae and humans who made up the troupe looked our way as Nadya clapped her hands.

"Let's put their skills to the test," she announced.

They made a circle around Reilley and me. Then Nadya handed Reilley a large hand drum. He sat on a stool and clutched the drum between his knees.

He started to pound the drum in a slow rhythm. I moved with the beat, smoothly swaying my limbs and torso. He increased the tempo, and I sped up, adding twirls and kicks.

Soon, everyone clapped to the beat. Reilley and I fed off the energy the other released. When we were finished, everyone cheered. Reilley and I shared smiles of admiration. Neither of us had known the other's talent.

"Well done," Nadya congratulated. "Next time, we'll put you in colorful skirts for an even better show." She patted me on the shoulder and went about packing camp.

"We're readying to leave," Andrei explained. "On to the next town."

Meeting Andrei's eyes, I felt drawn to him. His presence was like a forest sanctuary on a misty night: dark and damp from the mist, but refreshing, not chilling. The sanctuary provided safety, but mystery was hidden somewhere in the mist.

"What can we do to help prepare to move camp?" Reilley inserted himself in such a way to pull Andrei's gaze from mine.

"Why don't you get water since you know where the spring is?" Andrei suggested.

Reilley nodded and tugged at my sleeve. "Let's get the buckets, Em," he urged.

"I think you can handle that alone, can't you? Em, will you help me gather firewood?"

I stood at a crossroads, knowing this decision was more than water or firewood. "I'll help Reilley get water. Then we'll both help you gather firewood, Andrei."

Neither looked happy with the decision, but they didn't argue.

Reilley and I grabbed buckets and headed back to the spring.

"Are you all right, Reilley? You seem...different," I asked as I thought of him squaring off with Andrei.

"A lot has happened in a few days. Our crewmates are dead. I almost died, and you were put in serious danger. I still don't feel strong enough to protect you. I always thought things happened for a reason and that everything would work out in the end. Now, I feel lost."

I grabbed his hand and tugged so he'd stop walking and look at me.

"Don't lose hope, Reilley. Our crewmates are gone, but we're still here. *You* made sure of that. Don't despair if you feel lost. I'm right next to you. You know what I really need right now to get me through this trying time?"

"What?"

"A little Reilley optimism. I need you to believe everything will work out. I need you to smile brightly and warm me with some sunshine."

He took in my encouraging smile and returned to the bright-eyed Reilley who gave me the desire to keep going.

"I didn't know you could play the drum, Reilley." I changed the subject to a lighter topic.

"And I didn't know you could dance like the women I saw in Rome." His face turned red as he thought of something that clearly embarrassed him.

The cute expression was endearing, so I couldn't help but tease him a little. "I can do much more than that," I said suggestively and laughed as the lump in his throat jumped.

I went ahead to the spring, and he stumbled as he followed.

We retrieved the water and returned to camp.

Watching Reilley carry the water buckets, I noticed he was no longer the starving young man I'd met weeks ago. Regular meals and hard labor had filled him in with lean muscle.

I continued to watch him as we gathered firewood.

Self-conscious, he finally turned to me. "What?" he asked.

Shaken by the turn my mind had taken, I turned away to hide my embarrassment. "Nothing," I mumbled.

We finished gathering firewood just as the rest of the troupe was done packing up camp.

Nadya gathered everyone around to make formal introductions.

"Everyone, these are the newest members of our little band, Em and Reilley." Nadya gestured toward us. I bowed my head and tried for a smile. Reilley beamed and lifted a hand in greeting.

Then Nadya turned to Reilley and me. "You've already met Andrei; he's our troupe's 'illusionist.' Of course, our audience doesn't know it's real magic. You also know Meleana, I think? She and Viktor are acrobats."

The fit Fae with his arm around Meleana inclined his head, and Meleana smiled at us.

"Over here we have Selena and Endy with their daughter Eury. Selena reads fortunes. Endy sings, and Eury accompanies him on the lyre," Nadya continued.

Selena smiled serenely. Her skin was as pale as the moon, and her hair was dark as the sky it swims in. Her untamed eyes were a very unusual color of amber. Endy had luscious waves of brown hair and a handsome face. Eury, a girl just blossoming, stared at me curiously. She had her mother's dark hair and her father's pale eyes.

I don't think she has ever seen a half-Fae like herself. I met her eyes and smiled encouragingly, and she gave me a small smile in return.

"All right, let's move out. We should arrive in town tonight," Nadya said, and everyone headed for the wagons.

"Em, Reilley, why don't you ride with Andrei? I'll go with Meleana and Viktor," Nadya suggested.

Reilley frowned seriously at this arrangement, but he climbed into the wagon seat after me, putting me between him and Andrei.

"Ready?" Andrei asked once we were settled.

We nodded. He clicked his tongue at the horse,

and it started forward. Our wagon pulled up the rear, with Nadya's leading.

We sat silently for quite a while. Finally, the mystery shrouding Andrei pulled too hard, and I asked, "How long have you been with the troupe?"

"A few weeks," he responded shortly.

My skin itched under the weight of curiosity. I tried another approach, guessing.

"I imagine Viktor and Selena fled during the persecutions as they were in love with humans. Did you also flee as a human sympathizer?"

"No." He didn't take the bait.

I was getting frustrated at getting blocked. "How did you find them? Did you stumble upon them like we did?"

"No. Nadya is a relative," he said after a long silence.

I pursed my lips at my failure. *I'm not used to being curious about someone's story, let alone needing to be nice to get information. Reilley is an open book compared to Andrei. He'll tell me anything I ask. I don't trust Andrei. I just want to know.* I looked at Reilley. He watched the trees drift by but listened intently. *He doesn't know about Faerie politics. Surely, he noticed they were Fae as they weren't wearing glamours at camp. I should probably take the time to explain it when we're alone.*

"Why did you leave Faerie?" I asked directly.

"Why did you?" he countered.

I floundered for a response that didn't tell him who I was.

My silence unwittingly encouraged him to tease me. "As you said, Viktor and Selena left to be with humans and avoid persecution, but what about you? You've already told me that you and Reilley aren't lovers."

Reilley stiffened beside me, but he didn't turn his head.

"Is your human in Rome? Is that why you need to get there?"

Those queries did make Reilley turn. His eyes asked many questions. *Do you have a lover in Rome? Is that why I couldn't go to Rome with you last time? What did you have to take care of?*

Though Andrei's tone was teasing, he still wanted to know.

"No, I don't have a lover in Rome. I'm going to see an old friend, a teacher actually," I said to Reilley. His features relaxed

"Your turn," I urged Andrei. "Why did you leave Faerie?"

His misty night pulled me deeper as he shared a part of himself with me. "My parents thought I'd be safer here. They were discussing marriage with a certain woman's father. When she fell out of royal favor, they thought it would be best for me to hide for a while. I reached out to Nadya, and she told me where to meet her and the troupe."

"What of your betrothed? She must be upset she lost royal favor and you all at once?" I followed the markers he left for me on the dark path; each one shed a glint of light on who he was.

"She wasn't my betrothed," he explained. "My parents didn't tell me they were discussing marriage until they sent me away. I've never met her, but I pity her fate." He looked sad.

"Why? What happened to her?" Reilley asked, enthralled with the story.

"She was banished, ripped from her only family, and likely pursued into the human realm," he answered softly.

"Why was she banished?" Reilley asked.

"The queen declared her a human sympathizer."

"A human sympathizer?" Reilley wondered.

"Yes, since the queen came to power, many Fae have been banished to the human realm as human sympathizers. She's a major proponent of racial purity and feels too much interaction with humans taints the Fae. Of course, it's also a scare tactic that forces obedience. She kept the persecutions secret for a long time, threatening anyone who thought to tell the king. But now, King Frederick is dead, and her movement is developed enough that she won't be able to hide it much longer."

My heart ached at the thought of my father. "What about King Pika? Won't he try to stop it?" I grasped for information.

Andrei shrugged. "Maybe, but he's still young. By the time he comes to full power, it may be too late."

"If she's in the human realm, maybe you'll find her," Reilley hoped, wanting this love story to have a happy ending.

Andrei shook his head. "She's probably dead. I'm sure someone would've been sent to finish her off. Once the royal guards are after you, there's no escape. Even if she's alive, how would I find someone I've never met?" he despaired.

Reilley joined Andrei in sorrow.

"What's her name?" I asked Andrei.

"Princess Ember."

I felt like I'd been punched in the gut.

"Do you know her?" Andrei asked when he observed my response.

I didn't answer.

"Do you?" Reilley asked, unsure.

I nodded silently and turned to Andrei, searching his face in panic and wonder. *Papa never told me he was discussing my marriage. If Andrei is telling the truth, he must be from one of the four noble clans.* I licked my dry lips and whispered, "Are you from one of the four noble clans?"

"Yes, I'm the eldest son of the main branch of the Water Clan," he responded as though he was unsure why it mattered.

That would *put him in a position to marry the daughter of the king. I don't trust any of the Fae here, not after Charlie. But if Helena sent him, then he already knows who I am. And if Papa trusted him enough for me to marry...*

Andrei and Reilley nudged me with their eyes expectantly.

"I always preferred to be addressed as Ember."

Realization dawned on Andrei, and his untamed eyes locked with mine. Astonishment, curiosity, and something I couldn't identify stared at me from the depths that beckoned.

"Ember," Reilley whispered. "You're a princess?"

The sound of hooves clopping, the green light through the trees, everything was shrouded in the misty night of Andrei's untamed eyes.

"Ember," Reilley whispered, touching my wrist lightly with his fingertips.

"Yes?" I whispered back, eyes still on Andrei.

"Why didn't you tell me you're a princess? Why didn't you tell me you were banished or betrothed?" Reilley's hurt and confusion pulled me away.

I turned to Reilley and placed my hand over his. He looked at me, wanting any explanation that wouldn't be betrayal.

"Reilley, I didn't tell you I was banished because then I'd have to explain about my stepmother and who I am. I didn't tell you I'm a princess in order to keep you safe. The queen is powerful and dangerous. She wants me hurt, probably dead. Telling you would've put you in danger."

"I promised to protect you. Why won't you let me in? Don't you trust me?" he worried.

The ultimate loaded question. I remained silent for a while, searching his eyes for an answer. "Reilley, I trust you more than anyone else."

"Does that mean yes?" he asked, confused.

"It means I trust you as much as I'm capable."

He winced, and I prepared to shoulder the backlash. Instead, Reilley grabbed both of my hands. "What happened to you that you can't trust someone who'll never betray you? Who made you this way?"

Shocked, I responded candidly. "I've tasted the bitterness of betrayal many times. Each time I thought the person was worthy of my trust. I'm usually wrong. I can't even trust my own judgment. And when I'm not wrong, our bonds were destroyed in one way or another."

The many faces of the ones who'd betrayed me flashed through my mind: the servants and friends who'd acted as spies for Helena, those she drove away, and then there was Duncan. Lastly, Liam's face surfaced as the perpetrator of the ultimate betrayal, the one person who should've stood by me. A burning in the back of my throat and a tingling in my nose announced the oncoming tears. I coughed to keep them down.

"No," Reilley said firmly. He pulled me into his arms and buried my face in his chest. I didn't resist. "You're brave enough. I know, this time, you'll face your fear."

The tears poured into Reilley's shirt as I silently shook and clutched him.

"*I* will not betray you. You can trust me," he whispered into my ear and stroked my hair.

I'm afraid. I don't want Reilley to get hurt.

When the cleansing tears had run out, I looked up into Reilley's dragon-green eyes. The strength he projected made me see him in a new light. A flicker, which had started when he discovered I was Fae, bathed him in a glimmering glow. Looking at him in that moment, I felt like I'd been tending to an abandoned egg. I was so focused on keeping the egg safe from cracking that when it broke open, I assumed the hatchling would be a helpless bird that would continue to need much care. Instead, a dragon had been sleeping inside, growing into a creature capable of protecting himself and his loved ones.

I faced this fierceness in Reilley. "He isn't my betrothed. My father never told me he was discussing my marriage," I whispered.

His eyes sparkled as a smile spread across his face. "I trust you," he said.

Reilley's embrace warmed my wet cheeks.

The mist from a summer shower sprayed my face as I looked up into the dappled green light that filtered through the trees. The stones of the path were wet and slippery, but I splashed through the puddles happily on the way to our meeting place.

Crawling through a hole in the shrubs, I entered the forgotten orchard.

"Ora?" I called to my friend when she wasn't in her usual tree.

She stepped out from the shadows with downcast eyes.

I ran to meet her, smiling and opening my arms to embrace her.

She didn't return my smile and flinched as I reached for her.

I halted and dropped my arms. "Ora...what's wrong?"

"I hate you," she whispered.

My breath caught in my throat, and I couldn't respond.

She didn't raise her eyes as she continued. "I never want to see you again."

My nose and throat burned as tears welled in my eyes. "Why?"

She turned to leave, but I needed to know. I grabbed her wrist to stop her. She winced in pain. I let go, shocked that I'd hurt her. As she rubbed her wrist, I saw the dark blue bruise beneath her sleeve.

"What's that?" I demanded.

"Nothing." She quickly covered the offending welt.

I reached out before she could stop me and pushed up her sleeve. Bruises covered her pale skin. "Ora..." I gasped.

She snatched her arm away. "I wish I'd never met you." Her untamed eyes squinted accusations at me.

When she ran, I didn't stop her. My knees wobbled, and I collapsed in the wet grass, watching her retreating form. My tears flowed freely and silently as I saw yet another friend leave me.

A shadow blocked the struggling light, and I looked up to see who'd come to such a deserted place.

Helena's eyes glinted down at me with satisfaction. She smiled, and her tone was kind and full of pity when she said, "Did you think you were friends? The farmer's daughter wasn't very loyal, was she? You should be happy you found out before it was too late. It's so difficult to know who to trust."

I felt sick knowing Helena was behind Ora's injuries somehow. "Why do you hate me so much?" I asked her finally.

"Hate you? Why ever would you think I hate you? You aren't even worth such a strong emotion. You're a human speck who chains her father's heart. Do you think your presence benefits anyone here?" She lowered her voice to a whisper. "No one will ever want a wretched girl like you."

She smiled prettily, then turned on her heel. Her long, dark hair billowed behind her as she left me alone in my despair.

My heart ached at her words though I knew they were false. *Papa and Pika love me, and I have one true friend.*

I ran as fast as I could toward the gatehouse, slipping on the wet stones and skinning my knees and hands. The pain didn't slow me down, and I kept running.

I found Liam carrying firewood into his house. When he saw me, he smiled a welcome. Then his brow creased in concern.

"Ember, what happened?" He dropped the firewood, and I launched myself into his arms. He stroked my hair soothingly as he embraced me.

His golden comfort warmed my chilled bones until I was finished crying.

He waited patiently for me to calm, then pulled back to look at me. "You're hurt. Let's go inside and get you cleaned up."

I let him lead me inside by the hand and sit me on a kitchen stool. He went about collecting tinctures and bandages for my scraped knees and hands. When he was ready, he knelt before me and pushed the hem of my skirt up a little.

"Hold your skirt up so I can clean your wounds," he instructed.

I did as I was told but tried to hide my blush.

Liam didn't seem to notice as he applied a witch hazel-soaked cloth to my cuts.

The stinging made me hiss, and Liam's untamed eyes looked up into mine. My heart jumped, but I didn't look away. *I love you, Liam,* I said in my head. *I've always loved you.*

I'd never said it aloud because he'd never feel the same. We were childhood friends, which was reinforced when he said, "Don't be such a baby."

He went about cleaning and bandaging my wounds, and I watched him like a lovesick fool. I told myself it was enough that he cared about me. It was enough that we were friends, but a part of me worried about when it wouldn't be enough. Recently, I'd felt desires I didn't understand. I only knew I needed him.

Once he'd finished, he stood and looked at me seriously. "Now, tell me what happened."

"I wish our parents had arranged a meeting sooner," Andrei said. My eyes flicked toward him, startled by both his forgotten presence and his comment as he jolted me out of my memories. "The Water Clan could've protected you if the discussion had gotten to that stage. Neither of us would've had to leave home."

"The human realm isn't so bad," I replied.

"No, but I can move more freely in Faerie."

"Even on the run, I feel freer here."

"But had you joined the Water Clan, you would've been free," he pointed out.

"Perhaps, or maybe Helena would've destroyed all of us."

"The wheel is always turning. Our clan is the next to rule after the Fire Clan. The 250-year cycle will end eventually. She'd be foolish to go against us."

"She has destroyed many lives and killed many people. She wants power, and I'm sure her greed will eventually be her downfall. But remember, she was born to the Air Clan. She'd have their support as well. The Earth Clan may have sided with you, but an all-out war among the clans would be far worse than Helena just pursuing and tormenting me. I'd die before I saw so many lives destroyed."

"You'd die to protect the Fae?"

"Well, I'd prefer not to, but yes. We're so few compared to humans. We can't afford a war. Though I can't see how my death would help the Fae, I'd die to protect them."

Andrei sat silently, considering what I'd said. "You should've been queen," he proclaimed.

"No, I shouldn't have."

"Why not?"

"Andrei, I'm in-between, neither Fae nor human. Many would resist my claim, and that would cause upheaval. Most importantly, I don't want to be queen. Pika is intelligent and kind-hearted like our father. If he can rule without Helena, he'll be a much better ruler than me."

"There may be those who'd object your claim, but many would support it. I hope you're right and the king can rule unhindered before he's corrupted."

Pika has never been without Papa or me. I hope all we taught him holds true.

"In any case, I wish we could've met before we left Faerie," Andrei commented.

"I've only recently become someone worth meeting."

I looked to Reilley, who'd listened carefully to our discussion. The fierceness that had appeared lay dormant once more. He smiled at me brightly. "Well, I'm glad you came to our world."

"Me too." I smiled gently.

The wagons ahead of us slowed and stopped. Andrei pulled on the reins, and our horse stopped as well. Reilley and I looked to Andrei for an explanation.

"Lunchtime," he said, hopping down from the wagon seat.

Reilley and I climbed off, shaking the sleep from our legs.

"Who usually makes the meals?" Reilley asked.

"Nadya cooks, but we all gather the necessary ingredients," Andrei answered.

"I'll go help her," Reilley announced and started toward Nadya's wagon.

"I'll find water. Why don't you start the cooking fire, Ember?"

I nodded with more confidence than I felt. *I don't know if I can make fire on demand. Maybe Nadya has flint and steel I can use, just in case.* I grabbed some firewood from the wagon and headed toward Nadya and Reilley. "Where do you want the cooking fire?" I asked Nadya.

She pointed to a small clearing just off the road.

Arranging the firewood where she had instructed, I picked up a handful of twigs and stared at them intently. Concentrating, I whispered, "Ignite."

Nothing happened. I tried a few more times until I was too frustrated to focus.

"You should talk to Andrei." Nadya handed me a piece of flint and steel. "Fire and water may be different elements, but it's my understanding the training is the same."

"Couldn't you show me?" I asked her.

She shook her head. "I am not blessed with water."

I don't need another connection to Andrei. I feel too drawn to him already. I grabbed the flint and steel, sparked some tinder, and placed it just right for the wood to ignite.

Reilley and Nadya went about making lunch. Selena beckoned me to her wagon, and I approached with curiosity.

"Your dance will be much better with the appropriate attire. What do you think of these?" Selena pulled some garments from a trunk and held them up to me. In her hands glinted a flowing skirt of deep red with golden bells and discs sewn into the waist.

"It's beautiful," I said.

"And this." She handed me the skirt and held up a short top of the same color and design. "You can have them," Selena told me, holding out the top.

"Thank you. They're gorgeous," I said sincerely.

She smiled, placed both in a cloth bag and handed it to me. I went back to the wagon we'd rode in to put the bag away.

Andrei had just returned with two full buckets of water.

"Andrei." I grabbed his attention. "Do you have water?"

"Are you thirsty?"

"No, I mean do you *have* water?"

"Ah, yes. I have been so blessed." He placed the buckets on the ground and stared at one. "Flow," he commanded the water. It leapt from one bucket to the other.

Satisfied with his demonstration, I stepped closer so only he could hear. "Would you mind helping me? I only just got my fire. I don't yet know how to control it."

The cooling shadow I felt in his untamed eyes wrapped my anxious feelings in a soothing mist.

"I am at your service, Princess."

"Please, don't call me that," I said reflexively.

"Ember," he corrected.

"Thank you."

"When would you like to start?"

"As soon as possible."

"Very well. I'll give Nadya this water, and we can start immediately." He pointed into the forest. "About 200 feet that way, there's a stream. I'll meet you there momentarily."

I nodded and started in the direction he'd indicated.

I walked through the trees and came upon the stream. A large, smooth rock sat on the bank. The stream wasn't deep, maybe knee high. It was clear and revealed pebbles at the bottom.

I knelt on the smooth stone and eased my hands into the cold, clear water. I cupped a handful and drank, then I splashed my face. It washed away the tears I'd shed and left me refreshed.

Then I leaned forward and stared at the current as it flowed over rocks and fallen branches. The tinkling of the stream was reminiscent of the sound of the fountain in the palace garden.

***

I lay on the thick ledge of the fountain, listening as the water tinkled. Distant music and laughter filtered out of the ballroom as the annual Samhain ball commenced.

Too many people I didn't know, and didn't care to know, crowded the palace. I'd stayed long enough for the first few dances, and then I'd put Pika to bed.

He wanted to stay up to see all the people, but his drowsy eyes wouldn't allow it. I came to the garden rather than return to the ballroom.

"Your dress is getting wet, my lady," I heard a voice tell me.

I opened my eyes and sat. The fluffy skirts of my dress had indeed fallen into the fountain. I turned to face the young man who'd tried to save my dress. He was a groom, around the same age as me. He must've cut through the garden on the way from the servant's feast in the kitchens.

His tousled dark hair and jaunty, cavalier demeanor made me look more closely and smile.

"Thank you...what's your name? I don't believe we've met."

"I'm Colt, Miss. We haven't as I came here not long ago."

"Welcome, Colt. I'm Ember. Tell me, what're you doing now?"

"I'm free now, Miss. The other lads are tending the horses tonight."

"Please, call me Ember. What say we ditch this party and go on an adventure?"

Colt was all eagerness.

"Let me change, and I'll meet you by the well."

I rushed to my room, unnoticed, and changed into more comfortable clothes.

Colt awaited me by the well and smiled at my approach.

"Where are we going?" he whispered as I took his hand and led him into the brisk night.

We walked awhile through the trees until we reached a moonlit clearing. Silver light glinted from the grass and trees. I led Colt toward the center of the clearing and pointed up at the many stars. We lay next to each other in the chilled grass and wondered at the sky for a while.

Finally, I turned on my side and faced him.

"Colt." I got his attention, and he turned his head toward me. "Do you have a lover?" I asked directly.

"No."

"Have you had?"

"Yes."

"How would you like to spend the season with me? As you know, winter is cold and long. Do you want to warm each other?"

Colt didn't need much encouragement. He slowly reached for my hand, giving me time to change my mind.

A gentle touch made us ravenous.

15

A cool hand on mine brought me back to the stream.

Andrei crouched beside me with a wrinkled brow. He pulled his hand from mine when I opened my eyes.

The hunger I felt in my memory gnawed at my core. I latched onto Andrei's untamed gaze. Where Sasha had been hot, Andrei was cool, the type of cool that soothes your pains and beckons you deeper. The cool that makes you shiver once to readjust your body temperature, and you find the new temperature suits you better.

"Do you still want to learn magic?" Andrei asked, unsure of which path to take but not opposed to either.

I took a deep breath and let it out all at once. "Yes," I responded with a clear head.

He nodded and stood from a crouch. "All right, you know other types of magic but not elemental?"

I nodded.

"Elemental magic is in your blood and spirit. It's controlled with emotions and intent. If I'm angry with the intent to harm, the water will follow suit. If I'm playful, cheerful, sad, et cetera, the water will be the same and act accordingly. The key to controlling the water is being aware of your own emotions. If I'm angry but I need happy water, I make myself feel happy, usually by triggering happy memories. Then I visualize my intent and make my demand. Understand?"

"One, know what I'm feeling. Two, align my emotions with needed outcome. Three, visualize my intent. Four, make my demand."

"Yes. But it's not just knowing how you're feeling. It's the honesty that entails. You must be aware and honest with yourself."

No wonder my fire didn't manifest when I came of age. My emotions were on lockdown.

"Alignment is also difficult. Letting go of anger when you need cheerful flames will be near to impossible."

"I can see where that would be troublesome."

"Visualization is the same as with all magic. Though the more you work with your fire, it will seem as if it knows what you want before you even tell it. First, my teacher told me to mark my emotions throughout the day. One exercise that helped me is he would ask me how I was feeling at various times. I didn't have to tell him, but I had to make mental notes. Would you like to do that?"

"That might be helpful."

"Excellent. Lunch is probably finished by now. Shall we eat?"

I nodded, and we returned to the others.

"Hey, Ember." Reilley greeted me and handed me a bowl with meat, vegetables, and bread. I thanked him and sat by him to eat.

Eury asked Selena and Endy how they'd met. Selena told the story.

"One night, I came to the human realm by accident. It was Midsummer's eve, so the veil was thin. I was just taking a stroll, and I walked right through. There I was, walking down an unfamiliar path, when I heard a voice. The most beautiful voice I'd ever heard was singing about the moonlight on Midsummer's eve. I moved toward the voice and came upon Endy lounging among the roots of an enormous tree. He looked up as I approached and said, 'the gods have blessed me. They sent a Faerie maiden to me on Midsummer's eve. Are you lost, fair maiden?' Well, I thought he knew exactly who and what I was from the way he talked. I didn't know he was just giving, who he thought was a human woman, a compliment. I said, 'Kind Sir, I am indeed lost. Do you know the closest door through the veil?'"

Everyone laughed at the misunderstanding. Selena continued, "Of course, he was shocked to find out I was, in fact, Fae. I returned to that tree many times, and he was always there to sing to me."

Selena and Endy smiled lovingly at each other.

"What about Viktor and Meleana?" Eury asked.

We all looked at Viktor and Meleana to hear their tale.

"Our story is not so cheerful," Viktor warned.

"What happened?" Eury asked, hushed.

"He saved me from the Wild Hunt," Meleana

explained. Viktor wrapped a protective arm around her shoulders.

We all nodded our understanding.

"What about Ember and Reilley?" Eury turned to us eagerly.

"We aren't together in that way," I explained to Eury, who looked disappointed.

"Everyone finished?" Nadya asked, breaking the silence.

We cleaned our plates and put water on the fire. The horses were collected from where they were grazing and hitched to the wagons before we climbed in. Reilley got in before me, placing himself in the middle. The horse pulled, and we watched the trees go by.

Reilley seemed anxious about our first show. He asked Andrei many questions about how everything would work when we got to town.

As Reilley asked Andrei every question imaginable, I watched the light through the trees as we passed by.

Green light filtered through the trees as I playfully chased Pika. He squealed with delight as I scooped him up and tickled his belly. He giggled the carefree laugh that only children have.

"Caught you." I smiled at him.

His untamed eyes sparkled up at me.

"I bet I can beat you to the cave." He squirmed in my arms so he could start the race.

"I'll give you a head start," I said, putting his feet on the ground.

"Go!" He laughed as he ran.

I let him run ahead but never far enough that he was out of sight. I let him win, and he puffed his chest up with pride.

Putting my hand on his head, I ruffled his hair as he laughed up at me.

He retrieved the lantern we always left at the mouth of the cave. I cast a Fae light in the lantern and held it aloft.

He held tight to my other hand as we stepped into the cave. We didn't walk very far, just far enough that the outside light didn't reach. We followed the familiar curves of the tunnel until it opened into a large cavern.

We'd placed many candles around the cavern. Lighting tinder with steel and a piece of flint, I used it to light a bundle of twigs, then a candle. Lighting another candle, I handed it to Pika. Pika and I lit all the candles in the cavern. Then we sat against one wall and looked up.

The many crystals that made up the walls and ceiling reflected the flickering candles. The sparkling colors danced around us, and Pika's untamed eyes glittered with joy.

We watched for a while until I knew it was close to suppertime.

"Are you getting hungry, Pika?"

He nodded and rose to help put out the candles.

Upon exiting the cave, I noticed Pika held something in his free hand. "What's that?" I asked him as we headed home.

"I found it on the cave floor." He showed me a whitish yellowish crystal cluster. Small grains rubbed off as I handled it.

"Very nice." I complemented him and handed it back. "What are you going to do with it?"

"Let's put it in the fire and see what happens!"

I smiled at his usual response. "All right, we will after dinner."

We returned to the palace and ate a quiet dinner in a small dining room near the kitchens.

Our father was traveling around Faerie, trying to investigate elusive rumors of Fae persecutions. It seemed every time he heard of something happening, he'd arrive to find homes abandoned. Neighbors all claimed ignorance. The whole affair had discouraged him.

Helena hosted some party, which I was pleased to not be invited to.

Pika and I finished our pleasantly quiet dinner. On the way to his room, I borrowed a mortar and pestle from the kitchen.

I tucked Pika warmly into bed. He watched me start a fire in his hearth and grind up the crystal he'd found with the mortar and pestle.

"Are you ready?" I asked him, grabbing a handful of rock dust.

He sat up in bed and nodded excitedly.

I tossed the dust into the fire. We both watched in awe as the warm, yellow flames turned purple.

"Wow! How does it do that?" Pika asked.

"I don't know, but it's beautiful, isn't it?"

He agreed.

I tucked him deeper into bed as the purple effect wore off.

"Did you have fun today?" I asked him.

"I always have fun with you, Ember."

I smiled and kissed his forehead. Then I rose to leave.

"Wait," he called.

I turned back to him.

"Will you stay until I fall asleep? I don't want to be alone."

I nodded and sat near his head. His small hand held mine tightly until he drifted off to sleep.

I stared into the dying flames in the hearth. They cracked and hissed softly like the wind through the trees.

The wind made the branches of the roadside trees sway. The fond memory left me raw with homesickness. For a second time that day, I hoped Pika was all right.

Reilley seemed to have finished his inquisition as we stopped in the clearing outside of town to make camp for the evening.

Eury ran to take care of the horses. Selena glamoured the camp so no one knew we were there.

I threw myself into helping everyone else set up tents. "Where are we to sleep?" I asked Nadya.

"You and Reilley can stay in my tent again tonight. I'll bunk with Andrei. Tomorrow, you can each get a tent in town."

After setting up camp and collecting water and

firewood, we got ready to go into town to scope it out. Meleana and Eury stayed with the camp and the horses. As for the rest of us, glamours firmly in place, we started down the road into town.

Twilight fell as we walked down the dirt road. The setting sun glinted through the trees. Coming upon the first houses, I saw that this little village was much closer to what I remembered the human realm being like rather than what I'd observed upon my recent arrival. Some modern conveniences were present though, like the streetlamps, which flickered merrily.

The road became the town's main thoroughfare, and we soon came upon the town square.

"This may work as a space to perform," Nadya said while looking around the raised platform at the center of the square.

All the shops along the road had closed for the night except for the tavern.

"Andrei, Reilley, and Ember, why don't you see how the locals feel about outsiders?" Nadya pointed us toward the tavern. "Selena and Endy, head that way to see if there's a better place to perform. Viktor and I will go this way."

Andrei, Reilley, and I walked toward the only building lit up inside.

Opening the thick, wooden door, we entered a large room with long tables and benches. A fire blazed at the far end, and lanterns hung overhead. Some of the patrons drank quietly alone or with friends, and others were rowdy. The patrons nearest the door looked up at us as we entered.

"Take a seat wherever you like," the bartender called to us over the din.

We sat at the end of one long table near the door. Andrei sat next to a couple of merry looking gentlemen, and Reilley and I sat across.

A buxom girl with shiny curls came around to offer us drinks. She sized up Reilley and Andrei and settled on the latter. All smiles and dimples she was as she took his order and bent over to display her attributes.

Girl knows what she wants and doesn't waste time. I smiled at her bold manner, but Andrei wasn't biting. I don't know what he ordered to drink, but Reilley and I got the same.

Once she'd placed the drinks before us, Andrei turned to the fellows next to us as one of them spoke.

"Don't think young Rose will give up so easily, Lad," he chuckled to Andrei. "We don't get many visitors, and she's been dreaming of that long road."

They seem friendly enough.

"She'll be much happier at her warm hearth than with us," Andrei assured them.

"Just passing through?" the other asked.

"Perhaps. What do you have here by way of entertainment?" Andrei asked.

"Not very much I'm afraid. The nearest picture show is five miles. We usually come here to listen to ole Sean tell his stories. Sometimes, we can convince Clay to play us some tunes," the first man said.

"It has all gone downhill since our neighbors started making minte," the other man lamented.

"Our little town keeps getting smaller." The first nodded sadly.

"It sounds like you could use some entertainment to lift your spirits," Andrei commented.

"Couldn't we all?" the first man agreed.

Shiny Rose returned to refill our drinks and was disappointed to find we hadn't touched them.

"You must have an iron will to resist such enticing advances," the first man observed as Andrei remained politely distant from Rose.

"Not at all. My interest merely lies elsewhere." Andrei looked at me, and the two men followed his eyes.

My brow furrowed in surprise, and I felt Reilley stiffen next to me.

The two men smiled and nodded at me.

"Beg your pardon, Miss. How rude of us to assume. Good luck to you both," the first man said to me.

I opened my mouth to clear up this misunderstanding. Andrei stopped my explanation by standing.

"Thank you kindly, gentlemen. I do hope we see you again in the next few days."

We said our goodbyes and paid for our untasted drinks.

The cool night welcomed us as we left through the solid, wooden door.

We walked quietly with our thoughts toward the square. My newly-awakened emotions were jumbled as I felt the proximity of both Andrei and Reilley.

Andrei's misty intrigue beckoned me closer while Reilley begged me to stay. Reilley's fragility shone in the green stained glass of his eyes. My heart ached a little to see that insecurity resurface in him.

Comparatively, Andrei knew what he offered and did so with confidence. *Not to mention the assurance that Papa had encouraged the match.* The longing I felt to talk with my father surfaced once more. I stood alongside Andrei and Reilley on the platform of the square and closed my eyes.

"Follow your heart, little cub," I heard my father say in my memory as he had said many times before.

Great. Very helpful, Papa. Thanks. This was so much easier when I didn't care.

The uncertainty I felt begged for the numbness of the apathy I'd worn for so long. Then I pictured Indulal's serene smile and felt guilty for even thinking it.

I want to walk the misty, moonlit path with Andrei and discover his cooling depths. But Reilley is at a crossroads and needs my guidance. He could grow stronger and embrace the dragon's blood or shatter like a beautiful stained glass window, abandoned to the world. How long will it take? How long will Andrei wait? Which desire is the right path? Help myself as I've always done or help a friend? I have an entire life ahead of me. I need to consider what's best for me, too. Reilley is not my responsibility. He's a grown man. Is there a reason I can't help Reilley as a good friend would and explore Andrei?

I looked at Reilley, who met my eyes. What I saw in their jade depths was not something I was ready to confront.

Reilley had made some sort of decision that resulted in a shy, yet comfortable, demeanor. He had none of Andrei's self-assurance. Rather, he seemed resolute regardless of the result but unsure of what that result would be. He met my eyes straight with an admiration and affection that had previously been reserved for private moments of intense emotion.

I considered the implications of this change in Reilley until the others returned.

"Is this still the best place?" Nadya asked Selena and Endy.

They nodded.

"And what of reception?" she asked us.

"The locals seem hungry for entertainment. There's a larger venue in the neighboring town. However, considering Ember and Reilley just started, this will be good practice."

Nadya nodded in agreement. "Very well. Let's head back for the night. We will start advertising tomorrow morning for a show tomorrow night."

She talked about how we could make the space better for performing on the way back to camp, but my head was too full to listen.

Returning to camp, we all went to our respective tents. As discussed, Reilley and I went to Nadya's tent, and she bunked with Andrei. We had no cots, but we wrapped ourselves in blankets and lay on the ground.

"Goodnight, Ember. Sweet dreams." Reilley's eyes still sparkled with regard as we lay facing each other.

I hadn't felt the type of attention he was paying me since I received it from Liam long ago. It was different from just physical interest. It was as if he looked inside me and wanted to know more. I squirmed at the uncomfortableness of being truly looked at.

"Goodnight," I mumbled and turned to my other side.

It took a long time for me to fall asleep. My body was very aware that Reilley lay beside me, not an arm's length away. My heart pounded in my chest, and my skin radiated sensitivity, making every sensation feel significant.

This physical reaction to Reilley seemed foreign. My inner conflict made me feel as though my muscles were ready should I need to act. Confusion clenched my stomach, and I was unsure of whether that action would be to run or do something decidedly more frightening. I forced myself to remain still as my mind concentrated on Reilley's soft breathing. I unsuccessfully fought the illusion that I could feel his warm breath on my neck and face, knowing he really wasn't that close. The physical and mental strain eventually exhausted me, and I drifted into a fitful sleep.

16

"Ember," I heard Reilley whisper in my dreams.

"Hmm?" I snuggled deeper into the warm blankets.

"It's time to wake up," he persisted through the fog.

I cracked my lids and saw smiling green eyes not two inches from mine. My eyes popped in surprise to Reilley's proximity. I tried to sit quickly, but the blankets that entangled me foiled my plan.

"How late is it?" I asked while freeing myself.

"You have time to eat, wash, and change before we go into town to advertise."

Everyone was bustling around camp when I left the tent. Nadya directed Andrei and Viktor as they loaded a cart with props and such for the show. Eury cared for the horses in a glamoured paddock. Endy, towel in hand, motioned to Reilley to follow him. Selena waved to me from the cooking fire.

"Eat quickly, then we can have our turn to wash in the stream," Selena said as I approached.

I followed her instructions and ate. As we finished, Endy and Reilley returned, clean with wet hair.

Reilley's blond hair was a few shades darker and plastered to his scrubbed face. His emerald eyes shone all the brighter through the tips of his slightly curled hair. Drops from the tips dripped as he walked. He gave me a smile as a greeting, and I felt wicked for the thoughts that surfaced.

"Grab the red outfit I gave you. We advertise in costume. I can lend you bathing things until you can get some in town today." I barely heard Selena speaking to me.

I went to our cart and grabbed the bag with the red costume as she'd bid me. Then I trailed her, Meleana, and Eury to the stream we'd followed from the day before.

After removing our clothes, we stepped into the cool, clear water. It was chilly but not unbearable. We washed our hair and skin, then plunged into the stream to rinse off the soap.

We dried ourselves quickly with towels before we started to shiver. Putting on the flowing garments, I still wore my boots and dagger. Every step I took back to camp made bells tinkle at my hips. My torso was uncovered as were the tops of my breasts. Though I much preferred the comfort and practicality of pants, I felt cheered by the swish of the flowing, red skirt.

Selena had plaited my dark hair so the wet waves would not drip on my skin as they dried. The end of my braid brushed in between my shoulder blades.

We hadn't brought a mirror with us to the river.

However, the appreciation that sparkled in Andrei's eyes told me the costume suited me.

Reilley stared at me slack-jawed, then jumbled his words trying to compliment me. "Emb—you look...en-ench...wonderful."

I smiled sweetly at him. "Thank you, Reilley."

"Very good," Nadya praised. "We'll sell many tickets with you advertising. Everyone ready?"

Everyone else wore colorful costumes as well and nodded at Nadya. She made a motion for us to move out. Selena checked the glamour she'd cast on our campsite to ensure it was still intact.

Nadya and Eury drove the cart, and the rest of us walked into town.

Arriving at the square, Nadya handed me, Selena, and Endy flyers to pass around. Everyone else started improving the performance space with lights, props, and signs.

"Don't forget to smile," Selena told me as we split up to distribute flyers.

The townspeople were very receptive and seemed to look forward to our performance.

After all my flyers were gone, I returned to the square. The stage was coming along, and Nadya already had a line of ticket buyers.

I asked her if she could spare anyone to help me purchase tents and other supplies. She told me to take Eury. She also asked me to purchase a list of ingredients for future meals. She handed me a pouch of coins for the food.

I found Eury on the corner of the square calling to the crowd not to miss our performance that evening.

"Eury, would you accompany me to do some shopping?" I asked.

"Sure thing." She smiled and hopped off the platform to stand beside me.

Since I'd walked around the small town to hand out flyers, I already knew where I was going. First, we went to a shop that sold hunting supplies and purchased two small tents as well as blankets. As it was a lot to carry, we returned to the cart before buying the rest.

"Can I ask you something, Ember?" Eury said quietly as we walked.

"Sure."

"Are there a lot of people like us? Half-Fae, I mean. You're the only other one I've ever met."

"I'm not sure," I answered honestly. "In recent years, Fae who sympathize with humans have been persecuted in Faerie. It's hard to say how many there are like us if they and their parents are in hiding. We aren't the only ones though." I tried to be reassuring.

"Have you been to Faerie?"

"Yes, I lived there most of my life."

"What's it like?" Her eyes burned with curiosity.

"Much like the human realm was centuries ago. We don't have many of the devices this realm has. There are parts that are quite ancient and parts that are wild. We have towns and ruins where towns used to be. The most striking difference is that there is no separation from nature. Natural features, plants, animals, et cetera are everywhere you look even in your home."

"It sounds wonderful."

"It is beautiful but can be dangerous for people like us."

"How did you live there for so long then?"

"My father was very important."

"I hope I can go there one day."

"I hope one day it will be safe enough for you to go there."

After dropping off the tents and blankets, we went to purchase clothes and bath products for myself.

"Ember?" Eury said softly as I browsed the selections.

"Yes?"

"Do you have magic?" She avoided eye contact while fingering a bar of soap on the neatly organized shelves.

I turned to her seriously. "I did inherit magic from my father. However, I've been told it isn't uncommon for people like us to inherit only some, or no, magic from our Fae parents."

She cast her eyes down.

"But, you know, magic isn't everything. Being clever, savvy, and able to defend yourself comes in handy more often than magic."

"It does?" She perked up.

I nodded.

"How did you learn how to defend yourself?" she asked.

"I practiced by training with a childhood friend."

"Could you teach me?"

I smiled at her enthusiasm. "Of course."

I purchased what I needed, nearly spending all of my earnings from the airship. Then we bought ingredients for meals. We also got meat pies to bring to everyone for lunch.

The stage was ready for that evening. Eury and I passed around the meat pies, and everyone ate with satisfaction.

After we were finished, Nadya instructed Reilley and me to return the purchases to camp and practice our performance. Everyone else would give one last push to sell tickets.

We climbed into the wagon seat and rode back to camp. Along the way, Reilley smiled broadly but fidgeted as we chatted about what we should do on stage.

Reaching camp, we unpacked the purchases and set up our new tents. Reilley pitched his tent close to mine, and then we put away the food. He grabbed a small package from the cart and handed it to me.

"What's this?" I asked.

"I got it for you in town." He looked at the gift with bright eyes.

I unwrapped the brown paper and revealed a tambourine. It had a drum-like center with silver-colored jingles and red ribbons that flowed from a hole in the frame.

"It's beautiful, Reilley. Thank you."

He smiled slowly and let out a huge breath. I beamed back.

Clutching my new tambourine, I walked to a clearing to have more room to dance. Reilley grabbed the drum and started a beat. Like before, I moved to the rhythm. This time, my red skirt danced with me, and I shook my tambourine appropriately. We discovered that as long as I let Reilley choose the pace, we could improvise an entertaining performance.

We fed on each other's energy and ended at a natural breaking point, exchanging smiles as the last beat echoed off the trees.

"You're enchanting," Reilley complimented smoothly.

"I'm only expressing your music and following your lead."

He flushed with pleasure at the high praise.

"Could you do me a favor?" I asked him.

He nodded.

"Would you unplait my hair? It should be dry by now."

His eyes gleamed like I'd given him a gift, and I turned my back to him. With long, deft fingers, he gently unbraided my hair. Undone, he ran his hands through the soft waves to separate them. I shivered.

"Thank you," I whispered.

As his hands gently stroked the dark locks, I became aware that we were very alone. We'd been alone before, but this time was different. An air of anticipation settled between us. His hands stilled. Neither of us knew what should happen next, and the pressure quickly became uncomfortable.

"You ready?" Andrei entered camp suddenly. "You go on stage first."

Grateful for the interruption, we both rushed to get on the cart and head back to town.

We let Andrei sit between us while he drove. Dusk approached, and I quietly tried to let my thoughts drift away with the passing trees.

"What are you feeling now?" Andrei asked me to note my emotions.

Damn it. Of course he'd ask me now. Confused and a little disappointed. Surprised, I mentally shook myself.

"Confront the emotions. Don't bury them," he censured as he watched my reaction.

I gritted my teeth. *Confused by what has changed between Reilley and me. Disappointed that nothing has really changed at all.*

My heart pounded like Reilley's skilled hands on the drum. My own reaction didn't make sense to me. I'd never felt this nervous insecurity. I felt vulnerable. The last time I'd felt vulnerable was that last night with Liam in the courtyard. But rather than the heartbreak that accompanied that vulnerability, I felt anticipation, fear, and a hint of hope.

Though Andrei had encouraged me to face my true emotions, I couldn't handle them, or what they could mean, at that moment. I sealed them away and let the cool mist of Andrei's untamed eyes shadow my heart. My attraction to Andrei was straightforward. He was someone I could hide in, a cool, dark place where I didn't need to think. He could provide simple pleasure, and I could be myself without having to give part of me away. He promised I could remain intact for however long I wanted, a night or the rest of my life. A safe balance beckoned to me from his shadowy depths.

As we approached town, I set aside my feelings and prepared to go on stage. The rest of the troupe, minus Selena, was ready, and the crowd had begun to gather. When the audience was full, Nadya climbed the platform and called to them.

"Ladies and gentlemen, welcome to our show! We have a variety of acts to entertain and amaze you. Please welcome Ember and Reilley in their debut performance!"

The crowd cheered as Nadya exited and Reilley and I entered. Reilley sat on a stool in the middle of the stage with the drum clutched between his knees. I stood behind him, tambourine in hand, and waited for the beat.

He led the dance with his hands, and I followed. I twirled and swayed around him, slowing when he slowed and speeding up when he did. The connection we created and fed between us made me forget about the audience. There was only Reilley and the beat that drove me to move. As he struck the last note, and I struck an alluring pose, the crowd erupted in uproarious cheers. Some threw coins as Reilley and I bowed to them graciously.

We exited the stage, and Nadya returned to announce Meleana and Viktor. Endy, Eury, and Andrei congratulated us on our performance when we reached them.

"Where's Selena?" I asked Endy.

He pointed to a tall tent across the square. "She set up her fortune reading tent after lunch."

We all watched Viktor and Meleana tumble and get tossed about the stage as they performed their acrobatics. Reilley watched with glee, and the audience responded in all the right ways.

Endy and Eury performed next. Selena had been right. Endy had the sweetest voice I'd ever heard, and Eury's adept fingers on the lyre complemented her father's vocals in a way that made me weep.

The audience was appropriately awed and grew very quiet to appreciate each note. The roar that followed their performance sounded all the louder as a result.

Finally, Nadya announced Andrei, and he strode boldly onto the stage. His act was water manipulation. We knew it was real magic. The audience wanted to believe it was real but thought it all an illusion. I watched him masterfully command the water with envy at the control he had over his element.

"He really is good," Reilley admitted grudgingly.

I nodded in agreement.

When all was done, Nadya thanked our audience for coming and bid them have a good night. As the majority of the crowd dispersed, some people stuck around to share their approval with the troupe.

While thanking my admirers, I noticed that Rose, the tavern waitress, had made her way to Andrei. He thanked her graciously and excused himself.

She didn't appear to take the hint and followed after him. Feeling like he needed assistance, I trailed them to a dimly lit alley.

"I think I'm being straightforward enough, but if you need me to be frank, I will. Be my lover," I heard Rose say.

"I'm flattered, Miss, but I'm not interested," Andrei responded as kindly as possible.

"Why not? Do you have someone else?"

"That doesn't matter. I simply don't want to."

"Well, I just can't believe that. No one has ever said no to me."

Shit. I strode into the lamplight of the cozy alley.

"Andrei, I was wondering where you'd run off to." I swished my hips as I walked toward him. The bells at my waist jingled with every step.

Andrei tried not to look surprised as I stepped into his personal space.

"Who's this?" Rose demanded territorially.

"I'm Ember. Did you enjoy the show, Miss?"

"Who are you to him?"

"To Andrei? We're betrothed, isn't that right?" I looked to him to play along.

He nodded dumbly, and Rose smirked and narrowed her eyes.

I sighed inwardly. *You kind of suck at acting, Andrei.*

"Well, it was very nice to meet you, Miss," I said to Rose. Then I turned to Andrei and whispered loud enough for her to hear. "Come on, my sweet. You know how I feel after we perform."

I wrapped my hand on the back of his neck and pulled his head down to me as I stood on my toes. I kissed him hard and with feeling, the kind of kiss others feel uncomfortable watching.

He didn't resist and kissed me back passionately. When my mind surfaced enough to realize Rose had left, I pulled away. We both stared at each other, panting.

"That should keep her away," I said to fill the silence.

"Thanks for the help. She didn't understand rejection."

"I'm sorry it was so sudden. I couldn't think of anything else."

"I'm not."

The silence grew thick again, and we stared at each other in the dim alley with no one around.

"How do you feel now?"

"Like I want to do much more than kiss you, but I'm unsure of where that rabbit hole will lead me. Now, I'm irritated that my mind inserted itself in a situation where I've never needed it before, and I'm not sure it belongs," I answered aloud.

"Ah, you normally turn your mind off and ride the waves of physical pleasure?"

I nodded, not taking my eyes off his.

"Would you like me to cloud it for you? I have that ability, to shroud your mind in mist," he said softly.

"I know. Your misty depths have called to me since I first looked into your eyes."

He leaned down again until his lips hovered over mine. I could feel his breath on my mouth as he whispered, "Your choice."

My body knew what it wanted as my pulse increased with my breathing. I tilted my head back, ready to disappear down the shadowy path.

A gasp from behind yanked me back into the harsh light.

I looked over my shoulder and saw Reilley draped in shadow. His head was tilted in such a way that his blond hair shaded his eyes, so I couldn't see their expression. As I watched, his mouth closed firmly.

Unexpectedly, he strode forward and gently grabbed my elbow. His eyes still shrouded, in a raspy voice, he addressed me. "Ember, please come with me."

Of all the changes I'd seen Reilley undergo—the fierceness of the dragon, his vow to protect me, his determined look as he took on Simmons, his shy sincerity, or his battered face when he needed help— the way he acted at that moment scared me the most. I was more afraid for him than I'd ever been.

All thoughts of Andrei, and the oblivion he promised, flew from my head. I left him in the alley without a word as Reilley led me by the arm into the street.

Once he realized I'd follow him without help, he dropped my arm and took long strides down the road toward camp.

My limbs tingled with anxiety the farther we

walked in silence. Finally, when we were out of town and trees lined the road, I grabbed his hand to make him stop walking.

"Reilley, stop. What is it? Why are you like this?"

He stopped and turned to me.

"Why won't you choose me? I love you more than anyone else ever could. I'd die to protect you. Why do you choose everyone other than me?"

I stared at him in the dim moonlight, too dumbfounded to answer.

"You don't know? You didn't even consider me an option, did you?"

Not really, but not for the reason you think.

"Well, now you know. You can't help but consider me now that it's right in front of you." He stepped closer to me and took my hand; his eyes shone with devotion. "Ember, I love you. Please, choose me."

"Reilley," I choked. "I can't choose anyone in the way you want. My relationships just aren't like that." *I know I'm broken. I'm not good for anyone. Reilley, you deserve someone who can give you everything you give her.*

"I know you aren't good at trust. You don't have to choose now, but I want you to consider me from now on. I want you to know that I'll never betray you."

My heart stretched toward the hope that he was real, but my mind smacked it down before I could reach him. Conflict raged inside me.

"Will you think about me?"

I felt myself nod without making the decision to do so.

He smiled at me happily, having lightened the load of his emotions onto me.

I thought about how it had come to this and remembered leaving Andrei in the alley. "We should go back to town and help the others pack up," I said, turning around on the road.

Reilley followed me with a bounce in every step.

The rest of the troupe was still packing when we arrived. We helped, and I felt guilty for leaving the work for everyone else. As we packed, I found a moment alone with Andrei.

"I'm sorry for abandoning you without a word," I apologized sincerely.

Andrei looked at me seriously, then smiled playfully. "I'll forgive you if we can continue later on, *my sweet.*"

Even with Reilley's confession still ringing in my ears, I felt my body and mind pulled toward Andrei.

"Perhaps." I neither encouraged nor denied him.

We finished loading the cart and cleaning the stage and started toward camp. Nadya drove the cart and Eury slept beside her, slumped on the driver's bench wrapped in a blanket.

After arriving at camp, I tried my hand at starting the cooking fire again.

"How are you feeling?" Andrei coached.

"Exhausted."

"What kind of flame do you want?"

"The warm kind."

He chuckled. "All right, try thinking of a

memory that makes you feel warm or a memory of a particularly warm fire."

A warm fire.

I stared into the dancing flames of our cottage hearth. My parents cuddled in a large wicker chair behind me. My father hummed softly as he stroked my mother's hair.

"Papa, will I find a boy to love me like you love Mama one day?"

"I'm sure you will." He smiled at my daydreams.

"But how will I know if I love him back?"

"Follow your heart, little cub."

"But what if I don't know?"

"You'll know."

"But what if I don't?"

He continued to smile at me. "Do you feel the warmth of the fire on your skin?"

I closed my eyes. "Yes."

"That's how you'll feel when you look at the one you love."

"I hope I'll recognize him."

"As long as your heart is not chained, it will find him."

"What do you mean by chained?"

"I hope you never have to find out."

I closed my eyes again and let the fire warm my skin so I could recognize my love when he came.

I could remember the flames, and they filled me with warmth. I opened my eyes and stared at the twigs in my hand. Visualizing the twigs aglow, I whispered, "Ignite."

The twigs lit up with a gentle flicker.

I smiled up at Andrei, who grinned his congratulations. Then I put the twigs into the pile of firewood so we could start dinner.

Reilley cooked dinner so Nadya could count and portion our wages from the performance. Our pay wasn't bad. It replenished some of what I'd spent that day on clothes and supplies.

As we ate, Nadya talked to us about the next day. "Tomorrow, we'll head to the neighboring town. It's much larger, so we'll stay for a while. It's also more dangerous. I don't want anyone to wander around alone. There's a Fae safehouse, in the form of an inn, where we'll stay. The Fae there should be human sympathizers, but be careful regardless."

18

We arrived at the inn, which lay on the outskirts of town, early the next afternoon. The proprietor came out to greet us when we stopped outside. Nadya talked with her about where we could store our wagons and how many rooms we needed. The inn was busy, so she only managed to secure three rooms. The bargain struck, Nadya motioned for us to grab what we needed from the wagons.

"Peter!" the innkeeper called loudly.

A golden-haired Fae around Eury's age appeared.

"Take these to the barn for safe keeping," the innkeeper told Peter.

Eury watched Peter with stars in her eyes. She stepped toward him and quietly said, "I can help with the horses if you'd like."

Peter smiled at her with appreciation.

We all grabbed whatever we needed and watched Eury and Peter make eyes at each other.

Everyone except Endy smiled at them knowingly. Endy narrowed his eyes at Peter's back, and Selena rubbed her mate's arm soothingly.

Before heading to our rooms, Nadya called a short meeting. "We'll have to do some street performances to garner interest as we search for an appropriate venue. Split into groups to search, perform, and advertise. You can split however you like, but don't go alone. Feel free to keep any tips you get from performing on the street."

Dismissed, we went to drop our things in the rooms. I was sharing with Nadya and Eury. After washing quickly in the sink, I changed into my red costume.

I met Reilley and Andrei in the common room downstairs. Reilley had the drum strapped across his shoulders, and Andrei had two pouches of water at his waist.

The town was much bigger than the one we'd just left, but not as busy as the cities we'd docked in with the airship. We soon came upon a plaza surrounded by shops and bustling with foot traffic. It wasn't big enough for our whole troupe to perform there, but it was perfect for a small street performance.

"Why don't you go first? The drum will attract attention," Andrei said to Reilley and me.

Reilley beat the drum hard and slow to get people's attentions. I shook the tambourine and my hips to make the bells jingle. He pounded a rhythm, and I started my dance.

Many people stopped and watched. Some dropped coins into the pouch Andrei held out. I enjoyed performing on the street much more than on stage. It felt more intimate. I could see each person's smile.

After finishing our dance, Reilley and I took our turn collecting coins as Andrei amazed the crowd by manipulating the water from the pouches at his waist.

We switched back and forth, taking turns performing for passersby.

When dusk settled into the western sky, we split our earnings and went back to the inn. We'd earned a lot more at the previous day's performance, but the wage wasn't terrible.

The rest of the troupe had yet to return. We ordered dinner in the common room, sitting at a small table in the corner. We watched the many patrons at the other tables; most of them were Fae.

After the inn maid brought our food, I ate quietly while listening to a neighboring table's hushed conversation.

"I'm telling you, we may be able to go home soon. I heard that the boy king snapped at his mother the other day in front of a room full of people. They say he isn't happy with how she rules and means to seize the throne before coming of age," one Fae woman whispered to another.

"But how can he? He's too young," the other woman said.

"His uncle was around the same age when he took the throne."

"And look how that turned out for him. He married his childhood love and later discovered she couldn't provide an heir. So love-struck that silly boy was, he wouldn't even remarry when she died."

"Well, he doesn't have to marry right away though it might be a good idea. Then his mother couldn't maintain power."

"Oh, that one would find a way. You know, I heard she poisoned the lovesick king's queen. She was her lady-in-waiting, and she thought he'd marry her next. But, when he didn't remarry, he had to go, too."

"But the crown wouldn't have gone to her. The king had a brother."

"A brother whose human wife was mysteriously murdered, leaving him free to marry?"

The first woman gasped at her friend's insinuation. "No!"

Her friend nodded seriously. "Oh yes, and then that business about him dying, too. She never could control him the way she wanted. He may not have found out about the persecutions, but he never stopped investigating. And him bringing his half-Fae daughter to Faerie with him? Doted on that girl he did. They say that's why she initiated the human sympathizer persecutions in the first place. I heard he was talking to the Water Clan about his daughter marrying the eldest son."

"Really?"

She nodded.

Andrei and I looked at each other as the weight of their conversation settled upon us.

"Gossip and rumors," he whispered to me.

"Maybe, but I wouldn't put any of it past her," I responded.

Reilley watched us carefully, knowing that something was up. A clever light shone in his eyes as he put the pieces together.

Just then, Eury plopped down next to me, smiling like it was always sunrise.

"Isn't life wonderful?" she sighed.

"I take it you and Peter became fast friends?" I teased her, trying to put what we'd just heard away for later.

She blushed. "I hope we never leave this town," she prayed.

I stroked the back of her hair affectionately. "I hope he'll live up to your expectations."

She didn't seem to hear me, but Reilley did. He knew the comment wasn't directed at him. Still, he looked at me sharply, wanting to know who had let me down. I kept my attention on Eury, who pushed food around the plate she'd been given.

"Eury, you showed interest in self-defense yesterday. Would you like me to show you some tomorrow before we go into town to perform?"

"Yes, please!" Her eyes gleamed.

"All right, we'll start at first light."

The next morning, I woke Eury early and dragged her outside to a grassy space behind the inn.

She was an eager student and learned quickly. I showed her different scenarios of how she could be attacked and how she could counteract them. Then we practiced while I pretended to attack her.

When we were both sweaty and breathless, we returned to our room to shower and then met everyone for breakfast.

Nadya had recruited Andrei to help her search for a venue, so it was just Reilley and me for the day.

It was a marvelous day. I couldn't remember a time when I was so at ease. I'd become comfortable around humans, especially since I could cast an effective glamour. I found myself dropping my guard around Reilley without thought.

After his abduction, he'd become much more aware of his surroundings. We were able to share the burden of vigilance rather than me doing it all. The town we were in moved at a decent pace, but it had none of the chaos of that horrible place.

We spent the day performing and wandering around looking for a good venue. We looked in shop windows, laughed with the locals, and made good tips.

Reilley was kind to everyone, but he was especially good with children. He wasn't afraid to be silly with them, and I found myself laughing along.

"I like to hear you laugh." He smiled at me as he waved goodbye to a happy little girl.

"It feels like it has been a long time."

"Well, with me, you can laugh every day if you want."

The carefree atmosphere got very serious with implication.

It would be nice if this was my life. I looked at Reilley and smiled. Then my peripheral vision picked out a face I couldn't forget behind him. *My life will never be this happy.*

Golden curls shined in the afternoon sun. Reilley followed my gaze to the untamed eyes behind him, no glamour in place.

"Ember." Liam breathed in my presence like he'd just emerged from under water.

"What are you doing here?" I growled through gritted teeth. So many years of apathy toward Liam finally gave way to the rage it should've always been. My change in demeanor registered with Reilley immediately. He stood at my side and faced Liam. His dragon's heart pumped fierceness once more.

"You know why I'm here," he said. He took in Reilley's reaction and wrote him off as insignificant.

"She sent you, but why?"

"To see how you're faring in the human realm. There has been...unrest. She wanted me to make sure you aren't getting any stupid ideas about returning."

"I won't return. I'm exiled, and that's just fine."

"Good. I'm glad we could clear that up quickly."

"Is that all?"

"Yes."

"Liar. Why would she send pirates to kidnap me? And why would she send her most trusted dog to ask what she already knows?"

"Careful, Ember. That wasn't very nice to say. I didn't insult your pet." He motioned to Reilley.

Reilley and I stared icy daggers at him.

"Oh, we are touchy about that subject?" His mocking expression changed. "I volunteered for this assignment."

"Why?"

"I wanted to see you, of course," he said, like it should be obvious. "How I've missed seeing you every day. I really didn't think I would. I thought, surely, my heart wouldn't hurt quite as much as watching you bed every man who caught your eye."

I stiffened at the implication of me being unfaithful to him.

"Oh, I know. I was the one that broke us, but you didn't have to rub it in my face that hard. Regardless." Liam looked at me seriously. "I really do miss you, Ember."

The pain in his eyes was real, and my soul ached for my first love.

"You made your choice." I tried to sound resolute, but it didn't come through.

"Is there no hope left?"

"You abandoned me, Liam! And you helped her banish me."

He didn't respond.

How could he defend that when we both know it's true? I strengthened my resolve once more.

"Why are you really here?"

"She really did want me to check your resolve and make sure you were appropriately miserable."

"And the pirates?"

"The human-lover was becoming too fond of you and started having second thoughts. She thought she needed to mix things up a little. Was I surprised to see her rather than you! But, I must say, I was disappointed. I had such fun planned. Unfortunately, the time since then has given her a chance to rethink her strategy, so we won't get to do as I'd planned. But who knows what the future will bring?"

Oh Charlie, I hope you're all right.

"Why can't you just leave her alone?" Reilley confronted Liam.

Liam must've felt truly threatened because he lashed out. "What do you know? Do you think you know Ember? You don't know Ember. I've known her almost our entire lives! I loved her even when she flaunted her many lovers before my eyes. I've been there every step of the way and watched as she was kicked by the cruelty of her stepmother. I've seen her love, laugh, cry, and endure it all."

"That's where we differ. I wouldn't have stood by and watched, and I certainly wouldn't have helped." Reilley's rage burst at a volume I'd never heard from him.

Liam growled and lifted his hand to strike Reilley. I was there with my blade at his throat before the blow could fall.

"I see you're still too slow, Liam," I breathed in his ear as I clung to his back.

He dropped his arm and stilled.

"You tell your mistress that I have no intention of returning unless provoked through any action against me or mine. Do you understand?"

"I never did get to feel your legs wrapped around me." He leaned his head back against my shoulder, digging my dagger into his throat. His skin hissed as the steel of my blade made contact with his blood.

I climbed off his back and pushed him away. "And you never will again."

"Aw Ember, don't say that. Maybe she'll let me have you after she's had her fun. I'll take you even then. Even if you're broken." His untamed eyes turned truly wild, and his voice took on a deranged quality.

I cringed inwardly at the change in him. "Not going to happen."

He gave me a haunted look that made me wonder what else she'd done to the Liam I'd once loved. "She always gets what she wants."

"Not this time. You tell her to leave me alone, and I'll do the same."

Liam's lips twitched into a flat grin as his eyes sparkled mischievously. "I hope we meet again, Ember."

"I hope we don't."

I only let myself shudder once Liam had disappeared.

19

Once Liam was gone, I turned to Reilley. He stood firmly, unintimidated, and stared in the direction Liam had left.

When his green eyes, flashing like emerald lightning, met mine, I couldn't stop myself. I rushed to embrace him tightly, to prove to myself he was all right. He hugged me back and rested his cheek on my forehead.

"I can't guarantee she won't come after you," I told him.

"I know. But, if she does come after us, we can face her together." He tried to reassure me.

I don't know, Reilley. If she comes after me, I'd leave to keep you safe.

We returned to the inn early, not in the mood to perform. I didn't feel comfortable with Reilley out of my sight at the moment, so we sat quietly in the bedroom Reilley and Andrei shared until it was time for dinner.

Nadya said we'd stay in this town until we could

find a good venue. I itched to move on. *I don't know why I feel the drive to move. They have no problem finding me wherever I am. Moving will make no real difference except maybe protecting the troupe.*

Eury and I awoke early the following day. We were surprised to find Reilley at our usual practice spot.

"Do you mind if I practice with you?" he asked, unsure of his welcome.

I smiled at him gently, and Eury nodded her encouragement. I didn't say anything aloud because I didn't want to make a big deal of it. But inside, I was glad to see Reilley wanting to learn to defend himself, and I was proud he'd come to me.

We showed him self-defense exercises like the ones I'd shown Eury. He was a little awkward at first but looked determined and worked hard.

Eury and I both encouraged him as we returned to the inn to bathe before we hit the streets.

That day, Reilley, Andrei, and I made a serious effort to find a venue.

Andrei noticed our anxiety and the way we looked around. We finally told him what had happened the day before.

"Something is going on," Andrei said.

I agreed.

"What do you mean?" Reilley asked.

"Something has changed. Maybe those rumors about your brother's grab for power are true," Andrei guessed.

"Maybe," I mused. *Or maybe it's because she felt Eamonn break her binding spell, and the pirates didn't work.*

We didn't find anything that day, but we found the perfect space later that week. The day after, we brought the rest of the troupe. The space was an outdoor amphitheater in a park. Everyone loved it, and Nadya said she'd find out about performing there.

She ended up booking the performance a week in advance, giving us ample time to advertise and sell tickets.

The next week was a flurry of posters and flyers. We sold so many tickets that Nadya was hopeful we could stay for another performance.

The amphitheater was packed to capacity the night of the performance. Because this crowd was bigger and had paid more, each act was to be longer. As before, Reilley and I went on first.

The stage lights were bright. We couldn't see the audience, but I could feel something sinister watching among the cheering crowd. I told Andrei once we got backstage, and he searched the audience with me from the wings.

The audience was mostly human. Some Fae—like Peter, for instance—were there, but no one else we knew.

I was relieved when the performance ended and the audience dispersed. Disappointment struck in the form of good news when Nadya informed us she'd secured another show date in a few days.

As we packed the props and such, Andrei snatched my hand and pulled me away from the group to a shadowy alcove.

Tucked into the close space, I acutely felt his hypnotic pull.

"Last time, you kissed me out of necessity. I've thought of little else since. I've expressed my interest, and you've responded neither yes nor no. We know what our parents want, and I'm convinced we've met via serendipity. I can protect you from the fiends who chase you. All of that may be too big a question for now. Tell me, Ember. Do you have any interest in spending time with me? Would you like to get to know each other and pursue a possible future?"

"I've told you I feel drawn to you. You intrigue my body and mind. Yes, I'm interested in a possible future with you where I don't have to run and I can live peacefully. But I'm not certain about a lot right now. Would that cause unrest for others? Spending time with you now could be a bad idea for both of us. I just don't know what I want to do at the moment." I apologized for my uncertainty.

"I understand. You've been through a lot and have much to think about. Can I leave you a token to help you decide?"

I nodded.

The kiss he placed on my lips promised an entire realm of pleasure I'd never experienced. There was no mistaking my body's reaction to Andrei. When he broke from me, I yearned like an instant addict. One hit, and I'd be recovering for the rest of my life.

"Should you want to start to get to know each other tonight, I'll be at your service." He smiled wickedly. We both knew he'd caught me.

He left me dazed in the alcove, feeling the full impact of his absence. I tried to recover before rejoining the troupe but had little success. Every time I looked at Andrei, as we made our way back to the inn, my body ached. It was very uncomfortable feeling in the presence of others, especially as I was having a hard time hiding it.

I'm glad Reilley doesn't seem to notice. With that thought, no matter how I ached, I knew I wouldn't be going to Andrei that night.

I hadn't had that level of unsatisfied lust for many years. The spring that was so tight before Sasha relieved me was even tighter now. It was so bad that my erotic dreams woke me from a dead sleep. The fact that Reilley had done those things in my dreams made me feel dishonest.

The next morning, Eury asked to be excused from our sparring matches because Peter wanted to celebrate her successful performance. She was getting pretty good with a quarterstaff and had taken to carrying one with her at all times by strapping it to her back.

I smiled and told her to have fun.

The prospect of physical exercise alone with Reilley was all too easy to imagine. I walked slowly toward our meeting place, trying to clear my head of distracting and inappropriate thoughts.

Reilley stretching his long, lean limbs on the grass made all my efforts for naught. Images from my dreams the night before surfaced unbidden. I took a deep breath and blew out loudly, causing Reilley's eyes to find me. He smiled his good morning.

"Eury is celebrating with Peter, so it's just us today." I tried to sound nonchalant, but I was sure he could hear my heartbeat.

Reilley nodded his acknowledgment and shifted into a fighting stance. Eury and Reilley had been sparring for the last few days, and I only stepped in to demonstrate. While Reilley still had a lot to learn, he did seem more confident in his own skin.

I examined his stance and nodded, moving into a similar position. I let him try to attack a few times, easily blocking each attempt. Every few attempts, I'd move in slow, using an attack scenario we'd practiced to test his defense. He remembered all the defensive moves and executed them well.

After a while, we were working up a sweat, and Reilley's blond hair clung to his forehead.

Having just blocked a punch, I moved to counterattack. As I stretched out my arm to strike, the morning sun hit at just the right angle to make Reilley's eyes sparkle. It seemed like his eyes held the secret to every hue of green, but it was the green reminiscent of an enchanted forest that distracted me most.

My mind blanked as the unexplored wilds of the deep, green forest called to me.

Reilley pushed my wrist aside, causing me to lose balance. As I fell, fear prowled the forest. Reilley grabbed my arm to stop me from falling but pulled too hard and lost his balance in the process. We went down together.

I heard an "oof" from Reilley as we hit the ground.

I landed on top of him. His arms were wrapped protectively around me, my head tucked safely against his chest.

I relaxed from my instinctive flinch and looked at Reilley in panic.

"Are you all right?" we asked at the same time. Then we laughed.

I gazed into the forest of Reilley's eyes again, and everything got serious. My breath hitched as warmth spread in my core.

Reilley looked at me intensely. Then he took a deep breath and cleared his throat. He shifted his eyes and moved to get up. Seeing his purpose, I scrambled off him quickly and gave him space. He rose slowly, avoiding my eyes.

A thick silence choked us. Reilley's reaction to my heated look made me wonder. *Is Reilley uncomfortable with physical intimacy? Is he having second thoughts about his confession to me? I know he wants more than just a physical relationship. Is he protecting himself from getting involved with me before he knows my feelings? Or is he trying to be considerate and not press me before I'm ready to choose?*

I continued to stare at him, and he looked anywhere but at me. *Distracting himself or feeling uncomfortable?*

I put all my thoughts away for later and said, "Good job at blocking my punch, but don't try to catch a real opponent, all right?"

He nodded.

"I think that's enough for today. Let's get washed and head out."

He bit his lower lip and rubbed the back of his neck as he followed me back to the inn.

I was relieved to discover Andrei had already left with Nadya for the day. I didn't have the strength to be near him at that time in the state I was in. I would've avoided Reilley too if I could have.

I took advantage of Nadya and Eury's absence. I thought a little time alone would ease my tension, but my right hand was a poor substitute when I knew the heat of a willing man was within reach. Still, it took the edge off.

Reilley also seemed more relaxed when I met him downstairs. My mind took me right to images of what he'd been doing alone in his room.

And I'm right back where I started.

I thought the exercise of dancing would help. Instead, my movements, driven by Reilley's skilled hands on the taut skin of the drum, made everything worse. To make things even more intolerable, every time I looked at him, I felt a warmth that was reminiscent of a fire's glow. This feeling, which I couldn't manage to dismiss, was more uncomfortable than any gnawing heat in my core.

That night, I couldn't sleep, so I took a walk around the outside of the inn. I wandered around, lost in my thoughts and my hormones.

Behind the barn, I heard two men talking. I was surprised to recognize one voice as Reilley's.

"What is it you want from me?" Reilley's voice had that fierce quality to it.

"It's my understanding that you're Princess Ember's paramour?" the other man said.

Reilley didn't respond, but the stranger didn't seem to need an answer.

"What do you want?" Reilley repeated.

"I'm here to deliver the Faerie queen's ultimatum."

"I'm human. She isn't my queen."

"Irrelevant. Leave Princess Ember's company or you will die."

I tried to swallow my horror to hear Reilley's response.

"She can try. I'd rather die than leave Ember to you lot."

"Oh very well, let's try again. Leave Princess Ember or the queen will kill her."

Reilley grew quiet, and my heart sank.

"Ah yes, that's a different story, isn't it?" The stranger snickered.

"I do not accept," Reilley said firmly.

"Oh?"

"Tell your queen I do not accept her terms. Also, I'd be afraid if I were her. Ember warned that Liam guy to leave her alone, and her retaliation won't be pleasant."

"You refuse the queen's ultimatum?"

"I have faith in our abilities to protect one another."

"Very well, the queen will not be pleased."

"We can handle it."

Helena's goon promised to visit again on less friendly terms and left.

My reaction to that conversation felt strange. I wanted to laugh and cry, dance and fight, sing and scream. I felt many emotions at that moment, but the emotion that prevailed was the overflowing love that Reilley's faith and trust had unchained.

I ran around the barn to find Reilley standing quietly with his arms crossed and his eyes closed as he leaned his blond head back on the peeling wood of the barn.

I didn't muffle my approach. He looked at me when he heard my footsteps. Bewilderment shone in his eyes as I closed the distance between us.

"Ember, what are you doing h—?"

I cut his sentence short with my mouth over his. His emerald eyes popped wide with surprise, then cloud over. I kissed him stupid, pouring everything I felt into him. I made sure he had no doubt that I'd chosen him.

Breaking to catch our breath, Reilley shook off the haze. He wasn't satisfied with only physical love. He looked to me for an explanation.

Fine.

"Reilley, you may not be the strongest or the cleverest."

His expression said he hadn't seen that coming. But I wasn't blind to his weaknesses, and I wanted him to fully understand.

I continued. "But you're the kindest, bravest, most honest and pure-hearted man. Most importantly, you've shown that you truly trust me. Your unwavering faith has allowed me to embrace the feelings that have been brewing for some time."

I stepped closer to him once more. Looking up into his emerald depths that shone with love and joy, I said, "I trust you, Reilley."

"Do you love me?" he whispered.

I smiled up at him. "I'll spend the rest of my life showing you how much."

The amount of happiness that poured from him as he kissed me sweetly was downright unrealistic.

Though my inner spring was about to burst, I reined in my lust. *Reilley is untested in that arena. It's best if we go at a pace he feels comfortable. Besides, now isn't the best time.*

"Reilley, listen," I whispered urgently. "We aren't safe here. We need to go now."

"What about the performance?"

I didn't like shirking my commitments either, but I told him we had to skip it.

"Well, we can't just leave without saying anything," he said.

"You're right, but we can't have long goodbyes either. We'll have to make do with our roommates. It's still the middle of the night, and we have to get our things anyway."

I went to the room I shared with Nadya and Eury first and woke them gently. After thanking Nadya and apologizing, I turned to Eury.

She hugged me, teary-eyed.

"Listen, Eury. I'm going to make Faerie safe for you to visit. Until we meet again, follow your heart and keep practicing what I taught you."

She promised to be stronger than me the next time we met.

"I look forward to it." I hugged her once more, grabbed my bag, and went to Reilley and Andrei's room.

Reilley had already packed and was ready. Andrei waited for an explanation.

"What are you going to do?" Andrei asked.

"I'm taking her down. But first, I need to gather information and make a plan. So I'm going to see that old friend."

"Let me come with you. You know my family and I can help."

I met his eyes seriously. "I'm sorry, Andrei. I can't accept your offer or your help. She doesn't know you're involved, and I want to keep it that way. I don't want to start a war amongst the clans. Should I fail, I don't want anyone else to get hurt. It will just be a failed attempt by a lone assassin."

He understood even if he didn't like it.

"Reilley is going with you?"

"She has threatened both our lives. It's best we stay together." *I'm not going to bother explaining the rest of that story at the moment.*

He nodded. "Good luck. I hope we meet again in Faerie."

"See you in Faerie."

Andrei insisted Reilley take the drum in case we needed to earn money on the road. We thanked him and left the inn before dawn.

Having explored the town thoroughly over the last few weeks, we knew where the train station was. The train was slower than an airship but less expensive, and we needed to try to conserve our funds.

I'd never ridden a train before. I was amazed that such a huge, heavy vehicle could move on steam. As it whistled and rang into the station, Reilley explained how it worked.

We were safely in our seats when the train lurched and pulled us toward our destination. The scenery passed quickly outside the window, and I dozed on Reilley's shoulder for the short ride.

20

The train's whistle and bell jolted me awake as it pulled into the station. Reilley looked down at me affectionately as I sat up.

"What?" I asked.

"Nothing. You're just cute when you're sleeping."

"What are you saying? I'm not cute all the time?" I teased.

He donned a face of mock uncertainty like he had to think about it. I poked him in the side, and he laughed.

We disembarked and bought two more tickets. The train to London was full except for private compartments. They were more expensive, but we didn't want to wait for a later train.

We bought fresh bread for breakfast before boarding the next train.

The train compartment was rather cozy. It even had curtains to cover the windows. I closed the curtains on the rising sun. I curled up at Reilley's side, laying my head over his heart.

After a little while of the train chugging along, Reilley whispered softly, "What's going to happen?"

"I don't know exactly. I'm going to try to end this."

"How?"

"By killing the queen."

"Do you really need to kill her?"

I leaned back and looked at him.

"She has tortured people, killed them, and ruined many lives. This isn't a person who can live quietly in prison. Besides, she doesn't deserve prison."

"But what will happen to you if you kill her? Won't there be consequences?"

"Probably, but I can't let her continue to destroy Faerie. Reilley, this will be very dangerous. If you want, I can try to find a safehouse for you here. When I'm done in Faerie, I'll come back for you."

"No, I'm going with you no matter what. I'm just sad. We finally got together, but we may not make it out alive to enjoy it."

I understood the sentiment. I wanted a long future with Reilley, and it might never happen.

"I know," I whispered, reaching up and touching his cheek.

He turned his head and kissed my palm. His soft lips made my lust sit up and beg, but I beat it down.

Reilley looked at me with purpose and kissed my inner wrist. My core burst into raging flames.

"Reilley," I warned. "I'm not sure I'm stable

enough right now to help you through your first time."

"We might not have another chance."

Logic isn't helping.

Reilley slowly reached up and ran a fingertip along the ridge of my ear from tip to lobe. Like before, I shivered with pleasure.

"Reilley, do you know what you're getting into?" I panted.

"No, why don't you show me?"

His lustful eyes were too much for me to resist, so I gave in.

Though need gnawed at me, I soothed it with the promise of imminent satisfaction. That knowledge bought me time so I could gently guide Reilley. *The anticipation will make it that much better.*

I crooked my finger at Reilley to beckon him to me, and he hastened to comply.

I kissed him gently but with purpose, giving his blood a chance to heat up. Then I kissed down his neck. He moaned as my teeth grazed where his neck met his shoulder.

Pulling away gently, I removed my shirt and undershirt. I placed his hands on my breasts and let him explore. "Reilley, tell me at any time if you want to stop."

He answered me by rubbing my nipples with his thumbs. He was a quick study and took pleasure in making me pant and gasp.

He welcomed my hands on him as I unbuttoned his shirt.

I straddled his waist and carefully watched his reaction. It seemed his abduction was the furthest thing from his mind as he gloried at the sight of me on top.

Experimentally, he dipped his head to my breasts and discovered I enjoyed his mouth on me a great deal.

I knew he was ripe when his natural instinct made his hips rock beneath me.

I slowly reached between my thighs and cupped his manhood. He gasped, and I jumped, pulling my hand away.

"No." He guided my hand back. "Don't stop," he pleaded in a breathy tone.

Watching him gasp a second time, I saw it was in pleasure.

As it was his first time, I knew he couldn't last too long.

I stood and removed my pants and undergarments and sat on the bench across from him. He watched me, enthralled.

I slowly touched myself as he watched so he could learn what I liked. Bringing myself to the brink, I finally beckoned him to me.

He stood before me, and I unfastened his pants to reveal his hard cock. I looked up into his green eyes, clouded with anticipation as I brought the blunt tip into my mouth. After a few licks, his knees were ready to buckle.

I drew him from my mouth and pulled him toward me. He settled on top of me, and I moved his hips toward mine. Once I'd guided him inside me, his instinct took over. He thrust inside me, and I let him find the rhythm. We both moaned as he rocked his hips.

I was glad I'd primed myself because he didn't take long. Since I did, we were able to peak together with loud moans of fulfillment. He pumped inside me, then collapsed on my breast.

Stroking his hair, I kissed his sweaty brow. He wrapped his long arms around my torso and clutched me to him.

"Thank you," he mumbled into my chest.

I shook with laughter, and he looked at me curiously. I smiled and said, "Thank *you*."

He returned my smile and lay his head back down. We slept, satisfied and wrapped in euphoria, until we felt the train slow as we approached London.

We each took a turn in the tiny bathroom to clean ourselves as best we could. Then we dressed and prepared to leave.

I knew the emptiness that could follow love-making if a partner didn't reinforce the intimacy. I made sure to keep physical contact with Reilley as we waited for the train to stop in the station. I stroked his hair, kissed his face, and held his hand. He reveled under my attentions. Our first, and possibly last, time together would live in his memory not just as a meeting of flesh but of hearts as well.

I'm glad I could give him what I never had.

Returning to the city where we first met, Reilley and I fought through the crowd at the station. Discovering where we had to go next, Reilley said it was a trek to the next station. He hired a carriage to take us so it didn't take long to get there.

Once we arrived, Reilley bought sandwiches for lunch as I purchased two tickets to Dover.

We had a few hours before the train left, so I asked Reilley if there was anything he wanted to do.

He looked down at his shuffling feet. "Well, I'd like to visit my aunt."

I nodded. "Where does she live?"

"Not far."

We didn't walk far at all before we stood at the small, iron gate of a tall, skinny home.

Reilley hesitated at the latch, and I waited patiently for him to decide. Finally, he opened the gate and knocked on the front door.

A frail woman with dark hair and a dark bruise around one of her dull green eyes answered the door. She stared at us dimly for a few seconds before recognizing Reilley.

"Reilley?" She looked up at him in wonder.

"Aunt Margaret, what happened?" he demanded, staring at her bruise.

"Oh," she lifted her hand to her eye, "I wasn't paying attention and ran into a door."

Reilley squinted as he pursed his lips.

"Come in, Reilley. I'll make tea." She stepped aside so we could enter.

"Aunt Margaret, we don't want tea. I want to know what really happened. Did he do this to you?"

"I told you, Reilley. And please, let's not fight in front of strangers. Who is your friend?"

"This is Ember, and she isn't a stranger. Aunt Margaret, please, we aren't here for very long." He took her hands and stared at her seriously. "Did you really run into a door?" he pleaded.

She averted her eyes. "I just found out I miscarried again. He was upset. You know how badly he wants children. He didn't mean to."

Anger roared inside me as I heard Reilley's aunt excuse her husband's behavior.

Reilley sighed. "I thought it was me that upset him. Aunt Margaret, I'm sorry. I thought if I left, he'd stop."

My anger turned to rage, and I growled, "Where is he?"

Margaret's face paled, but Reilley answered, "At the club, probably."

"He won't be back." I turned to the door, not even knowing what direction the club was.

"Ember, no." Reilley blocked my exit. "Listen to me, the man deserves whatever you're planning for him, I'm sure. But, more importantly, we need to get my aunt to safety. Let the police do their jobs. Please, I need your help."

I looked over at Margaret. She seemed to have come to the horrifying realization that what had been done to her had first happened to Reilley and would no doubt be done to whatever children she might have with her husband. Her wide-eyed gaze skidded around the room, like she didn't know what to do.

"What do you need me to do?" I asked Reilley.

"Help her pack a bag while I make a few calls."

I grabbed Margaret's hand and told her to take me to her bedroom. As we walked upstairs, I heard Reilley talking into a strange device. "Yes? Operator? Please connect me to a boarding house for battered women."

In Margaret's bedroom, I hunted around for

travel bags. Finding some, I began filling them with clothes.

"Grab anything you don't want left behind," I instructed her.

She did as she was told, and I also made sure she took any money she'd been saving. Returning with full bags, we met Reilley on the ground floor.

"They're expecting you, and the police are meeting us there," he told us. "Are you ready, Aunt Margaret?"

She looked around, unsure.

Reilley's eyes locked with hers. "This is the right thing to do," he reassured her in a hushed voice.

That was all the push she needed. She grabbed her coat, and we carried her bags to the carriage that waited outside.

The carriage dropped us in front of a large building with several floors. Reilley knocked on the door, and a kindly woman answered.

"Ms. Southam? I'm Reilley Nai. We just spoke on the telephone about my Aunt Margaret." He indicated to Margaret.

Ms. Southam nodded. "Yes, please, come in."

She led us to a sitting room with chairs and couches, and we sat as directed.

"You are most welcome, Margaret. I understand that it is your husband who is the perpetrator. The police will be here shortly to hear your statement and photograph your injuries. We have everything you need to help you regain your independence and start a new path to a fulfilling life. You will have your own room and a bathroom, which you share with your neighbor. We work closely with psychological counselors for mental distress and career specialists to help you find a job. However, there are certain rules you must live by, which I can go over in detail later. For now, would you like to see your room?"

Margaret nodded.

We rose to follow, but Ms. Southam stopped Reilley. "I'm sorry, Mr. Nai. This is the only room male visitors are permitted in. You understand?"

"Of course, I'll wait here."

I looked at Reilley, and he nodded at me to go on.

After climbing two flights of stairs, we entered a room on the third floor. The room was small but efficient. It had a bed, a closet, a dresser, and a desk. There was also a small window.

"I will fetch you when the police arrive." Ms. Southam left us.

I started helping Margaret unpack as she took in her new surroundings.

"I was a terrible guardian to Reilley. Whenever he got hurt, he told me he fell or some other such nonsense. I was far too willing to believe his fabricated reasons. Even though I never saw my husband lay a hand on him, I should've known. I'm glad I didn't have a child. I would've failed it just as I did Reilley."

You're right. You didn't protect him. "You aren't the one who abused Reilley. Your husband did. It's best you remember that in the ordeals to come."

She nodded. "You will take care of Reilley, won't you?"

"Reilley is a capable, grown man. He doesn't need taking care of. But I promise to love and protect him to the best of my ability."

She nodded slightly with her lips pressed together.

"Hey," I said.

She looked up at me.

"No one has the right to treat you the way he did. You are your own person. You are strong. Now you have a chance to be who you want to be. Don't waste it."

She squared her shoulders and looked straight ahead with determination.

After we'd put her things away, we returned to Reilley.

"Aunt Margaret, will you be all right?" Reilley asked, grimacing.

She looked up at him. "I will be fine, sweet boy. Don't you worry. I'm strong." She smiled gently at us both, and her dull eyes shone a little brighter.

We said our goodbyes and promised to visit again. Then we left Margaret in Ms. Southam's care and went to catch our train to Dover.

21

R eilley was understandably upset about what had happened to his aunt after he'd left home.

"Reilley, what could you have done then? At least you were able to protect her in the end. She has a chance at a future now, and I'm sure he'll be punished though not enough if you ask me." I couldn't help but add the last part.

Still, he looked moderately soothed.

"Reilley, what did you do after you left your aunt's house, before you met me that is?"

"I was an apprentice to a musical instrument maker; he made percussion instruments. Unfortunately, business wasn't very good, so he couldn't afford an apprentice anymore. I couldn't find a job after that. I tried to stretch what little I had, but I eventually ran out. I hadn't eaten in a few days, so I asked some passersby if they had any food. They told me to give them money, which I didn't have. Their reaction is when you found me."

My soul ached with the hardship he'd experienced. I tried to draw his attention away from the painful memories. "I certainly didn't expect to meet my future love that day."

"I never even thought to hope for someone like you. You burst onto the scene like a firecracker. I didn't know people like you existed. You were so strong, so glorious. I would've followed you anywhere."

"Even though it was annoying at the time, I'm glad you did."

We shared a smile and got cozy for the remainder of the ride to Dover. It was dark by the time we arrived at the station. We hired a carriage to take us to the ferry port.

The ferry ran through the night, so we bought two tickets and boarded the boat. It wasn't like any boat I'd ever seen. It had two tall chimneys and a water wheel. Its whistle was deeper than the train's. Reilley told me it was a steamboat.

We stood on the deck and watched the lights from Dover fade. The cool night air whipped our faces as we stared over the black water of the English Channel. Eventually, we went inside to buy dinner from a café on board.

With full bellies and heavy limbs, we decided to rent a room for the night in Calais. It was easy to find a room at an inn near the port in Calais. We were so tired from our busy day that we climbed into bed and slept the way only exhausted people can.

We awoke well-rested the next morning and ate breakfast at the inn. Then we walked to the Calais train station and purchased two tickets to Lille.

Once on the train, we passed the ride in the observation car. The windows on either side of the car were so big, almost like the whole car was made of glass. If I didn't know better, I would've said it was magic.

In Lille, we had to walk ten minutes to another train station. There, we bought tickets to Paris. We ate lunch in the dining car en route.

While paying our tab, we counted how much money we had left.

"I'm not sure it's smart for us to go on to Rome to meet your teacher right away. We have money for food and maybe lodging. If we spend it on train tickets, we won't have any left," Reilley said.

"We'll just have to find cheap lodgings and make some more money before we go on."

We found inexpensive lodgings in the form of a hostel in Paris. We changed into performance clothes and hit the streets with our drum and tambourine.

Paris was a magnificent city. The streets were crowded with carriages and foot traffic. I also saw people riding on seats suspended between two wheels.

I tugged Reilley's sleeve. "What's that?" I whispered in awe as a rider whizzed past.

"That's a bicycle." Reilley smiled at my curiosity and enthusiasm.

We performed near a giant tower of iron that looked over the entire city. The tips were meager compared to what we'd been given before we'd left the troupe. Reilley guessed there were more street performers in Paris to compete with.

As night fell, the iron tower lit up with electric lights. It shone brightly like a beacon of inspiration.

We returned to the hostel, picking up an inexpensive meal on the way.

"We need a more effective way to make money," I said to Reilley, who lay on the bunk above me.

"I agree. It'll cost more money to stay here than to leave if it keeps going the way it did today."

We sat quietly, thinking.

"You looking for a way to make money?" A young man in the top bunk two down from ours looked over at us.

"Yes," I replied, a little suspicious about his sudden participation in our conversation.

"There's this man, says he's a scientist. He pays money to anyone who will help with his research."

"What do you have to do?" I asked, intrigued.

"He just takes a little blood and asks some questions, but he pays well."

"That doesn't sound so bad. Where can we find him?" Reilley inquired.

"That's the weird part. He's secretive about his research. I guess he's afraid someone will steal it. You know how scientists are. You get there through a tomb in Père Lachaise."

Okay. That's a little weird, but I am curious.

"What do you say, Reilley? Do you want to go on an adventure?"

The young man told us exactly which tomb it was and how to find it. He also recommended we go at night as he didn't seem to be there during the day.

The next day, Reilley and I tried more street performances with the same meager results.

At sunset, we went to Père Lachaise. It was like a hushed city with its cobbled roads and many residents. Though it wasn't cold out, I still felt chilled. The cemetery's stone mausoleums and whispering wind made the dead seem restless.

Following the young man's detailed instructions, we eventually found the tomb. It was a small, stone building with an iron lattice door.

The door creaked as Reilley opened it. Stepping inside, we saw only a stone coffin in the center of the room and a cord hanging from the ceiling to the left.

As directed, Reilley reached up and pulled the cord.

Nothing happened.

Feeling foolish, we turned to leave. The sound of stones grinding together stopped us as the coffin slid back, revealing a long, stone staircase.

I grabbed the lit lantern that hung from the bottom of the coffin with my right hand and Reilley's hand with my left.

He nodded his readiness in the lantern light, and we started down the stairs.

The bottom of the stairs opened into an antechamber. The walls were stone, lit up by cheerfully dancing lanterns. A rug beneath our feet muffled our steps. Similarly colored tapestries hung every few feet, attempting to bring warmth to the hard room. A large, wooden door with iron pins groaned open at the far end of the room.

A tall, pale man with chin-length, dark waves smiled at us. He wore a long, white coat. "Welcome," he said pleasantly.

Looking closer, I saw untamed eyes flicker

through his glamour. I dropped my glamour to show him that Reilley knew about Fae, and he dropped his glamour as well.

Reilley let out a relieved sigh. "Oh, thank goodness. I was sure you were going to be a vampire. What with the cemetery and having to come at night, not to mention the blood donation." Reilley turned to me curiously. "Wait. Do vampires exist?"

Before I could answer, the Fae scientist interrupted with great excitement. "Please, tell me you're here to help with my research."

"We're here to give blood and get paid for it," I replied.

"Excellent!"

"But first, I want to know what you're researching."

"Of course. Please, follow me."

We followed him through the wooden door with iron pins. The adjacent room was similarly decorated but had a few tables and chairs. One table had unusual metal instruments on it next to a chair that reclined.

He ushered us to two upright chairs on one side.

"I can't tell you how excited I am to have a half-Fae willing to help! But I'm getting ahead of myself. How many other half-Fae have you met?" he asked me.

"A few."

"Precisely. For as many Fae and human matings that occur, there aren't many children born. That's because not all humans are compatible with Fae. With the unrest in Faerie and so many Fae either fleeing or being exiled to the human realm, I believe the only hope for our species is to reproduce with humans. But how do we distinguish which humans are compatible from the ones that aren't? That is what I mean to discover. Also, some half-Fae possess the magic of their Fae parents and some do not. I mean to find out why."

"Very well, Sir, your research sounds worthwhile. You may have some of my blood," I said.

"Excellent! And, please, call me Dante. How about you, Sir? Are you a willing subject?" Dante asked Reilley.

"Sure," Reilley replied bashfully.

"Great! First, I'll take a sample from you, Sir. Meanwhile, Mary Ann will ask you a series of questions, Miss."

Mary Ann was a polite human with blonde hair and blue eyes. She entered from behind a tapestry and sat across from me as Reilley moved to the reclining chair.

"This will be kept anonymous," Mary Ann assured me as she asked my age.

"That's a complicated question. My age here or in Faerie?"

"Whichever."

"All right, I have celebrated twenty-six birthdays."

"Which of your parents is Fae?"

"My father."

Then she began to ask about my mother and her family. I told her I'd left the human realm centuries ago, and I was very young when my mother died. She settled for a physical description and the location of my birth.

"Do you possess your father's Fae magic?"

"Yes."

"Is he a member of one of the four clans?"

"Yes."

"Which one?"

"The Fire Clan."

"Which branch?"

"The main branch."

I was glad this human woman didn't seem to know much about Faerie and only posed the questions on her list.

"Do you have fire?"

"Yes."

This answer seemed to trigger a reaction in her.

"Dante?" she called.

"Yes, Dearest?" Dante answered as he finished with Reilley.

"Please, come here."

He crossed the room and looked at the paper with my answers.

Damn it. I didn't want him to know who I was until I left.

His untamed eyes were all enthusiasm when he looked up at me.

"A half-Fae blessed with an element? You are very special. Your mother must've been quite the human."

I was surprised he didn't mention my father having been king.

"Thank you," I said.

"Would you consider giving more blood? We'd pay double."

"How much would I be giving?"

"Not enough to make you faint."

I agreed.

Dante motioned me to the reclining chair as Mary Ann began to question Reilley.

Compared to the bloodletting I'd had as a child, Dante's small needle was practically painless. Setting aside the vials of my blood, he handed me two pouches of money.

Taking Reilley's and my blood to another table, he invited us to watch the initial compatibility test.

He grabbed a vial of blood and explained that it was his. Using a small glass tube with a squishy knob on top, he sucked a few drops of his blood into the glass tube. Then he held the tube over a metallic grey rock. He squeezed the knob, and a drop of blood landed on the rock. The blood fizzled and bubbled.

"Fae blood reacts acidically to iron," he explained. "That's why Fae feel repelled by iron. It doesn't harm us unless it comes into contact with our blood, but it is rather uncomfortable to be around."

He did the same procedure with my blood, and it reacted similarly though not as violently.

Finally, he dropped Reilley's blood onto the rock. Tiny bubbles appeared on the surface of the rock.

Dante looked up at us happily. "Congratulations! You're compatible for reproduction."

Reilley flushed beet red, and I burst out laughing.

Dante thanked us for our contributions, and we

thanked him for the money. We had more than enough to get us to Rome.

We bid Dante and Mary Ann farewell and good luck. Then we rushed back to the hostel, grabbed our things, and went to the train station. We made it just in time for a night train to Milan.

Locating our private compartment, we settled in for a long ride.

The train ride to Milan took all night and part of the next morning. For Reilley and me, it seemed too short as we tried to enjoy every moment we had alone together.

Once we reached Milan, we purchased tickets to Rome. Our final train left not long after we arrived, and we were back in Rome by mid-afternoon.

It didn't take me long to find the large amphitheater near the café. As Charlie and I had done, Reilley and I entered the café and found the old woman in the basement. This time, I could see through her glamour. I dropped my glamour and said, "Ciao, Nonna."

She didn't even look at Reilley, who wore the hat Charlie had given me pulled low.

"Ciao, bambina," she replied and motioned to the rug.

I was glad I remembered the way to Eamonn's as we followed the twisting tunnels. I tapped on his ill-fitting door quietly and prayed he was home.

"Who is it?" he called.

"An old friend," I replied.

"Come in," he instructed.

The relief on his face was easy to read as he embraced me.

"Ember, thank the gods! I've been so worried. You wouldn't believe the stories I've heard. Then, when I called and you didn't answer, I feared the worst."

"I'm sorry, Eamonn. The shell you gave me was lost in the sea when pirates attacked our airship."

"Pirates? You have been having adventures. I'm glad you're safe. Are you hungry? Thirsty? Who's your friend?"

"This is Reilley." Reilley removed the hat and bowed gracefully.

"It's an honor to meet an old friend of Ember's, Sir," Reilley said.

"Now, just who are you calling old, Lad?" Eamonn said sternly.

Reilley's mouth gaped open, and his face paled. Eamonn and I laughed.

"I'm only teasing, my boy. Would you like something to eat?" he asked us.

"Please, allow me," Reilley insisted and began puttering around to make food.

Eamonn and I sat at his small table.

"This has gone on long enough, and I mean to stop her. Tell me what you've heard is happening in Faerie."

"I've heard many things. It seems your brother wants to seize power before he comes of age. She's panicking. She thought she had more time to choose an easily-manipulated bride for him, but he's insisting he will choose his own. Very strange, he ordered a large fire be kept burning on a nearby hilltop for all to see. They say the flames burn purple."

"Pika," I choked on sudden tears.

"Does this mean something to you?"

I nodded. "It's his way of telling me to come home."

"Then he's expecting you. Perhaps she is as well, and that's why the portals are now guarded."

"Perhaps."

"Also, that friend of yours who you brought with you last time, it seems she's being held captive."

"Charlie? Where?"

"On the outskirts of Earth Clan territory."

"Right, we'll rescue her first. Do you know anyone who can help us get in unnoticed?"

He nodded. "I know a Fae who can smuggle you into Faerie."

Reilley set plates of food in front of us and sat down. We thanked him and began to eat.

"Eamonn, I've been thinking. You know that seal Helena put on me to block my magic? Is it possible to place a protective seal on Reilley? One that would give him Fae-sight to see through glamours and other protections against Fae magic?"

"I'll see what I can do."

After we ate, Eamonn wrote something on a piece of paper and handed it to me. "Go to the market and inquire after Hawnt, give him this, and bring him back here. Reilley and I will stay here and work on this Fae-sight and shield question."

I kissed Reilley on the cheek and went about my errand, pulling my hat low. I found the weapons vendor I'd visited before and asked him where I could find Hawnt. He pointed me to a tavern down the way. After asking the bartender, I found Hawnt drinking at a small corner table. He was a scruffy-looking Fae with keen eyes.

I sat across from him and placed Eamonn's note on the table between us. He read it and looked at me curiously. Then he downed the rest of his drink and stood to follow me. He didn't speak the entire way to Eamonn's. Once we were inside, he bowed to Eamonn humbly and didn't straighten until Eamonn placed his hand on Hawnt's head in blessing.

"What can I do for you, Sir?" Hawnt asked in a gruff voice.

"Hawnt, I need you to get these two to Faerie, undetected, near Earth Clan territory."

"Is that all, Sir?"

"And tell no one of this, eh?"

"Of course, Sir."

"When can you be ready, Hawnt?"

"In a few hours, Sir."

"Excellent. Return here to fetch them when you're ready."

Hawnt nodded and left. Reilley showed me the knotwork shield Eamonn had cast over his heart.

"Eamonn, that reminds me. The original reason I came to see you was to tell you I got my fire."

Eamonn's eyes widened, and then he smiled broadly.

"Have you learned to control it at all?"

I told him what Andrei had instructed me to do.

"Brilliant suggestions. He must be quite the water user, or he had an excellent teacher. Keep practicing, and I have no doubt you'll learn to control your fire flawlessly."

In the hours before Hawnt came to fetch us, Eamonn drew a rough map of where we needed to go to rescue Charlie. He also told us how to find people who'd support us while in Faerie and gave us a small lantern to light the way. He wrapped us each in a cloak with a deep hood to help shield our identities.

"One more thing before you go. You and Reilley must stay together. I see great misfortune should you split up."

We nodded our understanding. With that, a knock sounded on the door. We grabbed only necessities, leaving the drum and tambourine with Eamonn. I hugged Eamonn once more and promised to see him again. Then we left through the ill-fitting door.

Reilley and I followed Hawnt in silence through the dark twists of the tunnels. The path we followed eventually led us to what I guessed used to be a cellar. It was difficult to tell what it used to be exactly because the walls and roof had crumbled long ago.

We saw the night sky above us as we exited the tunnels and crept around the ruins of an ancient city. I didn't know whether it was war or just time that had brought these once magnificent buildings crashing down, but I mourned their destruction and longed for their glorious past.

We climbed the hill the ruins clung to, unwilling to let go but not strong enough to be raised to new heights. Hawnt led us to a clump of foliage watched over by tall, skinny trees with leaves only at the very tops. Hiding among the shrubs, Hawnt summoned a door to Faerie.

"This is an unusual place for a door," I commented.

"Most doors to Faerie are guarded, but some are ancient and forgotten," Hawnt explained.

Reilley eyed the portal uncertainly. It shimmered and sparkled like moonlight on rippling water.

I took his hand. "Are you sure about this?" I asked.

He squared his shoulders and nodded. We stepped through the veil together. It felt like rubbing velvet over bare skin.

We entered another ancient place. The thick stone of Faerie ruins were covered with moss. The hushed night made every footstep, every breath, sound too loud and too close. Old trees guarded the long forgotten ruins. Their gnarled roots enveloped the moss-covered stones in their safe embrace. Tall and thick with age, they still spread their many leaves toward the starry sky.

While the night of the human realm was lit by lamps and electric lights, the forest we entered was aglow with spirit lights, the spirits of lives passing through the realm or content to spend time there. Their soft, green lights faded in and out as they floated in the ancient wood.

Reilley watched them, fascinated. I tugged at his hand, and we followed Hawnt through the forest. Our progress seemed slow. With every step, we remained surrounded by the thick silence. When we found the tree line, we stuck our heads out and saw the small, but solid, building where Charlie was being kept. We thanked Hawnt for getting us in and went our separate ways.

The building where they were holding Charlie was dark and imposing. Torchlight illuminated the entrance and the guard. Like every prosperous house, there was another entrance for those who were to remain unseen, the servants.

Normally, servants protect their entrances with great pride for the family that pays and protects them. However, since Helena became queen, the outrage of masters mistreating servants had gone unpunished. Creeping through the trees, Reilley and I made our way to the servants' entrance.

Eamonn had explained that many in Faerie craved my brother's ascension to the throne as the lone ruler. They hoped he'd bring an era of peace.

Removing the small lantern Eamonn had given me from my bag, I cast a purple Fae light.

Approaching the servants' entrance, we quietly knocked on the door. The peephole slid open, and I held aloft the new sign of hope for my brother's rule. The peephole closed, and we heard quiet clicks as the door was unlocked.

I turned the knob and gently pushed. The door opened without a sound. We entered a kitchen large enough to feed the household and its guards. A plump woman with pale cheeks stood in the dark kitchen, a flickering candle in her hand. Two kitchen helpers, a boy and a girl, slept in a small bed of straw in the corner.

"The purple flame burns brightest," she whispered.

"It announces the rising sun," I replied as Eamonn had told me.

The plump woman smiled at us.

"We're here for the prisoner," I explained.

She pressed a palm to her heart and smiled softly. "They put her in one of the cellars. A guard stands outside her door."

"Only one?"

She nodded. "We don't have many guards to begin with. And, while the queen wants her imprisoned, she doesn't seem terribly important to her."

I turned to Reilley. "It may be better if you stay here."

"Not a chance. You heard what your friend said about staying together." Reilley's expression left no room for negotiation.

There will be no explaining to Reilley that Eamonn always worried too much and had many visions of misfortune that never came true.

I nodded. "Which way to the cellar?" I asked the woman.

She explained how to navigate the cellars and wished us good luck.

So we didn't implicate the kitchen lady in our prison break, Reilley and I didn't use the kitchen entrance to the cellar but quietly left from the door we'd come by to ensure it was locked behind us.

Not far from the servants' entrance, another door led to the underground cellars. As the woman had said, the door was unlocked to allow for an easier changing of the guards. Descending the stairs, a long hallway with other hallways and doors leading to other cellars stretched before us.

I was convinced I was going to have to incapacitate Charlie's guard, but—from the sounds of grunting and moaning echoing off the walls—that seemed unnecessary. We snuck swiftly past two comrades enjoying each other's company. It seemed to be an exchanging of the guards as one guard had another bent over a table meant for aging cheese. Lucky for us, they were facing the other way.

Don't mind us, boys. Carry on.

We continued down the hall until we found the door the woman had indicated. Clearly, they were only thinking of keeping Charlie in because the lock was just a bar of wood across the frame. I lifted the wood and placed it to one side. Then I quietly opened the door.

The room was pitch black and smelled of filth. Bitter cold made me shiver, and I could hear shallow breathing.

I cast a Fae light in my lantern. The dim glow illuminated a figure huddled in the corner. Charlie's untamed eyes looked up through grimy hair.

I lifted my finger to my lips to tell her to be quiet. Then I motioned for her to follow us. She tried to stand but couldn't put weight on her ankle. I helped her climb onto Reilley's back.

We shut and locked the door behind us and snuck past the guards, who were still at it.

I wish I could hear the explanation those boys give their superiors when they find Charlie gone.

I smiled as we climbed the cellar stairs and disappeared into the surrounding wood.

23

Once we were at a safe distance, we paused to take a breath.

"Ember, Reilley." Charlie's voice cracked with emotion. "Thank you for coming for me."

"Don't worry, Charlie. We're going to take you back to the human realm," I reassured.

"No!" she protested too loud.

I hushed her. "Charlie, you need to see a healer."

"I'm not leaving Faerie without Johnny."

"You're in no condition to rescue anyone. We will find him."

"Ember, I can't leave without him. They may kill him before I can get back. Besides, I know where he's being kept. My brother has him, remember? You'll need me to navigate the place. Just find me a healer here. We have no time."

I understood Charlie's desperation. *I'd do the same.* "All right, do you know this area? Where can we find a healer?"

"There's a village not far from here." She pointed deeper into the forest.

We found the road through the forest and headed in the direction she'd indicated. We soon came to the village. The windows showed no light. Everyone was asleep. Some of the houses, however, had small lanterns hanging by the doors. A purple Fae light glowed with hope.

We approached one such cottage on the edge of the village. I tapped at the door softly. After a few moments, a disheveled man cracked the door.

"The purple flame burns brightest," I said.

"It announces the rising sun," he replied and opened the door to let us in.

"Sir, thank you for opening your home to us. Our friend is injured. Do you know a healer?"

His wife entered the room in her bedclothes and went about making a fire in the hearth.

The man nodded. "I'll go fetch her." He left.

Reilley set Charlie down gently in a chair.

"Thank you for your hospitality and help, Ma'am," I said to the woman, who handed us each a cup of tea.

"There was a time when it was common to help each other," she said.

"I hope to see that time again," I replied.

She nodded in agreement.

Her husband soon returned with a healer, a young woman, who looked like she'd been pulled from sleep. She went right to Charlie without a word.

"Thank you for coming, Miss," I said.

The healer nodded her acknowledgment and

went about treating Charlie. "She needs rest," she instructed as she finished.

For all her lack of pleasantries, her care of Charlie was exemplary. She left as quietly as she'd come.

The man and his wife didn't have room for all three of us, but they offered a bed to Charlie and a hayloft in the barn to Reilley and me. We gratefully accepted their kindness, made sure Charlie was comfortable, and went to the barn. Climbing the ladder to the loft, we settled in the hay above two horses and a cow.

I lay on Reilley's chest as he stroked my hair. "Do you think Johnny is still alive?" Reilley asked.

"I don't know. I hope so."

He held me closer. "I can't imagine the pain of losing you."

I squeezed him back, but it didn't feel close enough.

That night in the barn, our lovemaking was slow and expressed a desperation to exist only in that moment with each other.

Charlie slept most of the next day as Reilley and I helped our hosts with chores. We chopped wood and weeded the garden.

By nightfall, Charlie had awoken and bathed. She looked like her old self though a little thinner. She was more than ready to rescue Johnny. We thanked our hosts and let Charlie lead the way. We had quite a walk to get to Charlie's family home.

"What happened to you since we last saw you?" I asked as we hiked. "Do you feel comfortable telling us?"

"It may be easier to show you," she said, reaching out her hands to Reilley and me.

I ran past the bow of the pirate ship to make sure they saw me in Ember's guise. *I have to get as far away from Ember and Reilley as possible before the pirates catch me.* I really tried to get away, but a pirate soon tackled me to the ground and hauled me back onto the ship.

He put me back in the cell in the cargo hold.

"Should we go after the others? I think we could make quite a profit," the pirate that had caught me said to the captain as he checked to make sure I was secured.

"No, this one is worth twice that. The Faerie queen must want her something fierce to offer such a reward," the captain said. "Don't worry, Missy. You'll be home in no time."

I paced around the cell like a caged animal as the ship gained altitude.

The pirates won't hurt me as long as they think I'm Ember. But whomever the queen sends will be Fae, and they'll be able to see right through my glamour. What will her agents do with me? Or will they let the pirates keep me?

The sound of shouts and shots rang out on the deck above. There were scuffles and thuds. *Did a fight break out?*

Suddenly, the ship started losing altitude.

The cargo hold door opened, and Sasha rushed down the stairs.

"Sasha, I thought you were dead!"

He unlocked the cell and hugged me fiercely. It took me a second to get over his physical intimacy. *He thinks I'm Ember.*

"We agreed to join the pirate crew until we could find the right time to escape," he explained. "I am so glad you are safe."

He kissed me with enthusiasm right on the mouth. I pushed him away and changed my glamour to the one he knew as me.

"Charlie?" His confused expression demanded an explanation, but the ship lurched and began falling faster.

"What's happening?" I asked.

"The envelope was hit during the fight. Mac is trying to land the ship, but we might crash."

We raced to the main deck, stepping over pirate bodies bleeding on the floor.

Mac held tight to an antique ship's wheel. I looked up, and Sasha was right. Hot air was escaping from a hole in the envelope.

There's no fixing that.

The best we could do was hold onto something as we crashed into the ground. At least Mac had managed to crash into a field.

I'd held onto a railing during the impact. The actual crash felt like it took a long time before it was over, but it couldn't have been longer than a few seconds. As I got to my feet, I looked around the wreckage.

"Mac! Sasha!" I called.

"Here," I heard Mac call from the direction of the ship's wheel.

I made my way through the twisted metal and splintered wood and found him pinned under the broken wheel.

I moved it off him and helped him up. He seemed unharmed.

"Sasha!" we both yelled.

"Da!"

Sasha had been thrown from the ship and had landed in the field. He had some cuts, but nothing seemed broken.

Now that we knew everyone was all right, they turned to me for an explanation.

"I thought it was Ember that the pirates recaptured," Mac said.

Sasha grunted. "Me too."

"I'm Fae. I can change how I look to humans. More importantly, do you know where the pirates were supposed to take Ember?"

"Yes, but why?" Mac asked, clearly not satisfied by my explanation.

"I have to go there instead."

They both refused.

"You don't understand. The person after Ember is determined. She needs more time to get away. If I go there and pretend to be her, it may buy her that time."

"Ember is still in danger?" Sasha asked.

"Yes, and this will help her."

"I am in," Sasha agreed.

"No." Mac still refused.

I forced Mac to look at me. "Mac, listen. Ember is in danger because of me. I betrayed her by spying on her. I need to do something to help her. Please."

Facing my pleading eyes, Mac reluctantly agreed.

The field we'd crashed into wasn't too far from the inn where the pirates were to meet the queen's agent. We walked as quickly as we could, but we were still late.

I glamoured my appearance even though I was sure the agent would be Fae, and covered myself with a cloak I'd found in the wreck.

The agent was waiting for us in a private room at the back of the inn.

"You're late," he said as we entered.

Sasha held me by the arm like I was a prisoner, and Mac stepped forward to talk.

"We had trouble finding the place," Mac explained.

I kept my face pointed at the floor and hid in my hood.

The agent rose from the table he'd been sitting at and approached me. He ripped off my hood, but his smile of anticipation turned to scorn.

"You aren't Ember."

I looked up at him. His golden curls shined in the firelight.

"Yes, I am," I tried to bluff. *Maybe he doesn't even know Ember.*

He snorted like he'd know Ember anywhere. "You're the human-lover sent to spy on Ember."

Well, shit.

His shoulders slumped, and then he glared at me. "You'll pay for betraying us," he growled and grabbed me by the arms.

Mac and Sasha tensed to defend me.

He eyed them.

"Don't!" I told them.

They stilled.

"I'll go with you," I told the agent.

No matter what he does to me, it will cost him time, time that he won't be looking for Ember.

He grabbed my arm and dragged me out of the inn. I looked behind me to see Mac and Sasha clenching their teeth but following my wishes.

Charlie released us from the shared memory.

"Then the agent took me to the prison where you found me," she summed up the rest.

I was so relieved to find out Sasha and Mac were alive and beyond grateful that Charlie had given herself up to Liam to buy us more time.

I hugged her tightly. "I'm sorry I got you into this. Don't worry. We're going to save Johnny," I promised.

We continued toward our destination as she told us the layout of her family's house and where Johnny was likely to be.

Charlie's childhood home was much like every distant branch families'. It was a complex with a main house and many smaller buildings for guests, food stores, and the like.

"My brother has a small building to himself for his projects and whatnot. I think that's where he'd keep Johnny," Charlie said as she pointed to one building.

"Will there be guards?"

"Not likely. He'll rely on the complex guards, and he'll have him locked up."

"Where will your brother be?"

"He always sleeps at the main house."

"So we have to get past the complex guards, rescue Johnny, and get out?"

Charlie nodded.

"Too easy." I smiled. "But if we should get separated, meet at the nearest door to the human realm. Where is it?"

Charlie pointed deeper into the forest behind us.

"Be careful," I advised. "It may be guarded."

We slunk to the complex wall closest to the building Charlie had pointed out. The wall was not too high. Reilley gave Charlie a leg up and boosted her to the top of the wall. Then he boosted me. We reached down from the top of the wall and pulled him up. Then we all landed gently on the other side. Hearing a patrol guard coming, we ran to a nearby shed, where we hid inside until he passed.

We rushed to her brother's building. The door was locked, but Charlie knew where he hid the key.

The trouble with siblings is they know your secrets.

By the side of the door, there hung a bell. Charlie carefully took down the bell so it wouldn't make a sound. Turning it over, we saw that the clapper of the bell was a key. She unhooked the key and used it to unlock the door. The building was a home in its own right. We passed a staircase, which no doubt led to bedrooms. We walked through a sitting room and into a kitchen. Then we crept down creaky stairs to a basement.

After lighting a candle, I couldn't believe what we saw. A thick, wooden table was stained with dark, dried blood. Another had instruments of torture. Chains hung from the ceiling with manacles at the ends. Similar chains ran along the floor. It was too easy to imagine a man held aloft, spread-eagle.

More chains secured a man against the far wall. He was filthy, crusted with dried blood and grime. His clothes hung in tatters on his starving frame. Cuts and sores were visible on his skin, and it was clear they hadn't been allowed to heal. His face was swollen and bruised as he flinched up at the light.

"Johnny!" Charlie sobbed and rushed to him.

Reilley and I looked around for something to break his bonds.

"Charlie?" Johnny croaked.

I found a big hammer and a stake on the table of instruments. The sound of metal on metal rang out as I used them to break his chains.

Reilley and Charlie helped Johnny up the stairs, and I readied my dagger for anyone who might've heard the ruckus.

We were almost to the door when we heard footsteps on the main staircase.

"Oh Charlotte, I knew I should've just killed him. Maybe then, you would've come to your senses," a man with similar features to Charlie mourned.

24

I guess he doesn't always sleep at the main house.

Charlie looked up at her brother, rage burning in her eyes. "Clint, I will never forgive you."

His face twisted in an expression of pain at his sister's harsh words. "Charlotte, don't say that. I did this for you. Don't you understand? The queen is considering you as a potential bride for her son! Can you imagine that from a distant family branch? Only this human stands in the way."

Wow. Helena sure has him in the palm of her hand. Charlie wouldn't have been considered a potential bride for Pika the moment she had second thoughts about spying on me.

Charlie shook her head at her brother in disgust. "Goodbye, Clint."

Clint flew into a rage and rushed at us.

"Go!" I yelled at Charlie, Johnny, and Reilley. "I'll hold him off and meet you at the door."

I blocked Clint from following them as they headed for the front door. I kept my dagger at the ready but didn't want to use it if it could be avoided. *Charlie may be angry at her brother, but that doesn't mean she wants him dead.*

We sized each other up, neither of us moving.

He made a swift lurch toward the door, and I blocked his way.

"So I will have to deal with you first?" Clint asked in a hard tone.

I nodded, steeling myself for a fight and waiting for him to make the first move.

He launched into his attack. He was quite good, well trained, but I was still better. I blocked each attack but didn't counter. I just needed to stall for time.

His face reddened in frustration when he couldn't land a hit. Clearly, he was accustomed to being the best. When I thought enough time had passed, I said, "It's too bad you're such an idiot. I think we could've had fun sparring together."

I landed a well-placed kick to the side of Clint's head and fled.

I climbed a tree near the wall and jumped to the other side. Then I ran to the nearest door to the human realm, where I quickly incapacitated the guard and waited for the others. Charlie and Johnny eventually hobbled to the door.

"Where's Reilley?" I demanded.

Charlie looked over her shoulder. "He was right behind us."

Panic rose in my throat. "All right, you go on ahead, I'll wait for him."

I made sure they were through the portal, then

sped back to the complex. I watched for a long while, knowing he'd have to come that way.

Finally, I crept close to an entrance. I couldn't hear a commotion inside, so I moved even closer.

"Hey!" A guard spotted me.

I turned to run.

"We have a message for you," he called.

I froze, confused, and took the paper from the guard's hand. It read:

Princess Ember,

I seem to have acquired a replacement human to play with. I spoke with the queen. She bids me tell you, "If you wish him to live, come to the palace and exchange your life for his."

Might I add that you make haste? Humans lives are so fleeting, you know, and yours is as delicate as a moth.

I hope we meet again soon.

Yours truly,
Clint

Bile rose in my throat, and I vomited as sorrow made my stomach clench. *Helena has Reilley. She will do so much worse than what Clint did to Johnny.* "Reilley," I sobbed and fell to my knees. "I'm sorry."

I wallowed in misery as determination wrestled for control. Eventually, I steeled myself for what needed to be done.

I asked the guard where the closest place to hire a horse was, and he helpfully pointed me to a nearby village.

I knew Helena would send agents after me even if she'd invited me. She wouldn't want to take any chances that I'd come up with a plan while making my own way to the palace. Hiring a horse was simple enough, but taking the time to feed the horse and let it rest while I took back roads was agony. I knew they had a head-start, and I'd never catch up to them. Clint had a carriage and could ride nonstop by changing horses along the way.

Every moment that passed with Reilley in danger made me want to vomit again, but I didn't let myself fall to pieces. Reilley needed me strong and ready, so I ate and slept to keep my strength up.

The second night on the road was the worst. I prayed some unforeseen delay had hindered Clint's arrival as I knew they would have already reached the palace at the pace they could go. I settled among the thick roots of a massive tree, having given the horse food and water and tethered him to a low-hanging branch.

I willed myself to sleep by picturing a cherished image of Reilley's even breathing as he lay in Nick's bunk. The image shifted as I drifted to sleep.

Opening my eyes, I saw Clint smiling gleefully up at me.

My wrists and ankles were in manacles, and I stood at the center of a room. One lamp sat on a table with menacing instruments and dimly illuminated the corners of the cold room made of thick stone.

Liam sauntered up to the bars that acted as one wall of the cell.

"Clint, you haven't started yet, have you?" Liam asked.

"I was just about to."

"Well, don't. Queen Helena has given him to me for the time being."

"What? But it was my guards who apprehended him. I brought him here!"

"You're to return home and await further instructions."

Clint snorted and stalked from the cell. Liam entered and stood where Clint had just been. He was taller than Clint and could stare me directly in the eyes.

"So, Reilley, was it?"

I didn't respond, but he went on anyway.

"Don't worry, Reilley. I'm sure Ember is on her way to fetch you now."

Ember, please don't. Run away.

Still, I knew he was right. Ember would never leave me. An odd combination of relief and panic made my heart jump.

Liam moved close to my face, his nose a few inches from mine.

"Do you think you love her, Reilley? Do you know what love is? Let me tell you. Love is giving up everything you've ever wanted so she can stay alive. Love is suffering through the pain of knowing you've betrayed her and watching her change into someone completely different to survive that betrayal, all so she can remain breathing. I've endured every tear, every glare, every frown and, worst of all, every look of indifference. I even fought the desire to flee my home with her because I knew, if we were found, it would be that much worse for her. You cannot imagine the things I've done to protect her. Tell me, Reilley, would you have done any of that? Could you have?"

I pitied Liam. He was so broken, clinging to the tatters of a love he'd destroyed. If he had truly known Ember, he would've known she would rather die for love than live without trust. He ripped that trust from her, and he couldn't forgive himself.

"Don't you dare look at me with pity, Human. It is you who will lose in all of this. Ember will be mine again, and you'll be broken and alone."

"Ember's free to choose," I said finally.

"She is. Do you think she'll choose you after you're mangled beyond recognition? Queen Helena instructed that I keep you in one piece physically... for the time being. She didn't mention that your mind remain thus."

Liam raised his hands to my head and stared into my eyes with intent. I stared back, unable to look away.

The skin above my heart grew warm. The warmth spread across my entire body. I felt like I was submerged in a hot spring.

Liam's intense expression changed to one of frustration. He released my head and began searching my body. He examined my neck and arms before he ripped open my shirt. He squinted at the shield over my heart with disgust.

"Sometimes, she's too clever for her own good," he mumbled. "No matter," he declared.

Liam walked to a lever on the wall near the bars and switched it down.

The chains attached to my arms and legs rang in their rings as they pulled taut. My arms were forced over my head, lifting me off my feet. My legs were spread wide, and my shoulder and hip sockets screamed under the strain. I clenched my teeth against the pain.

Liam perused the instruments of torture at his disposal and decided to start simple with a many-tailed whip with barbs at the ends.

I heard it crack, and the pain followed soon after. The skin on my torso ripped and began to weep. A scream fled my throat without permission.

Liam smiled with satisfaction.

Ember...I love you...

I awoke in tears, shaking as I sobbed. I let myself cry until I fell into an exhausted sleep.

25

It took another day and night to reach Fire Clan territory. The time passed in a blur of numb determination.

Nearing the palace, I saw the great purple flames Eamonn had described. *I hope Pika won't be there to witness whatever happens.*

I removed the horse's tack and released him to find his own way. I slipped onto the palace grounds over the crumbled wall near the willow where I used to meet Duncan.

The palace was a series of stone buildings. Some had branches and roots that grew around the outside, engulfing them like a casing. Some had natural springs that welled into fountains. Streams of golden green light filtered through the trees and played on the white stones and shining fountains.

Having snuck around the grounds for most of my life, it wasn't difficult to creep amongst the outer buildings and make my way to the main hall. Reaching my destination, I climbed up the roots and branches of a tree, which hugged the side, and jumped down onto the balcony.

The small library was deserted as expected. It was little more than an organized storage room as most of the prized books had been moved to the much larger library my father had built across the palace.

It appeared as though no one had been in there since I'd left Faerie. Of course, I was really the only one who'd visited it before I was banished. I ran my fingers over the dusty volumes of stories about when humans and Fae lived together. Sometimes, I'd curl up by the fireplace when it was cold and rainy and read them until I fell asleep. Other times, I'd stand on the balcony, or climb the tree and look at the moon and stars. But most of the time, I'd use the forgotten library as a cover so I could sneak out and not be missed.

I crossed the room to a small desk and grabbed a quill from the top of a stack of papers. The inkpot beside it was dry with neglect, but I found a bottle of ink in the drawer. After dipping the quill into the ink bottle, I pulled a blank piece of paper toward me and closed my eyes.

Visualizing my desired result, I opened my eyes and wrote:

Open

I crumpled the paper and reflexively turned toward the cold fireplace. *Right, I can make my own fire.*

Taking a deep breath, I tried to remember what

Andrei had taught me. I didn't really care what kind of fire I made as long as it burned the paper. *What am I feeling? Desperation. Frantic flames fueled by desperation would probably burn down the whole building.*

Thinking of how it felt as I lay in Reilley's arms only a few days before, a warm glow spread through my chest. I stared at the crumbed paper in my palm and imagined it as ashes. "Ignite," I demanded.

A flame consumed the paper in a flash, and a bookcase built into the wall slid aside to reveal a spiral staircase. Rubbing the ashes from my hands, I descended the staircase and stood before a two-way mirror.

I stared through the glass into the throne room where Helena and Pika sat on thrones made of living trees as Liam stood to one side. It seemed as though someone was making an appeal to the king as an older Fae of humble appearance knelt on the floor before the thrones.

After a while, he rose and bowed to them, and a guard showed him out. When the guard shut the throne room door, I slid the mirror aside and stepped into the room quietly.

I cleared my throat, drawing their gazes. Pika rose from his chair in surprise. He'd grown taller than me in my absence. A smile lit his face as he met my eyes.

"Ember, you received my message!" He moved to embrace me, but I held up my hand to halt his approach.

"I did, Pika, but that isn't why I'm here."

He flinched, then tilted his head to the side.

I turned to Helena. "Prove to me that he's safe and will remain so, and I'll do whatever you ask."

Helena nodded to Liam, who left the room and returned with Reilley in chains. He fastened him to the floor where the accused stand trial.

"Ember, you shouldn't have come." Reilley struggled against his bonds.

I sucked in breath as I raked his body with my eyes. I'd hoped the vision was just a horrible nightmare. I shivered in fury as I took in the welts and bruises, and I squinted my rage at her.

"Well, Liam was being such a good boy. I had to let him have a little fun. He's alive anyway," Helena explained nonchalantly. Her untamed eyes glinted playfully.

Liam smiled, pleased with his work. "You know, I tried to get in there and play in his mind, but that shield really is effective. I settled for physical punishment and telling him all about our great love story."

"What is the meaning of this?" Pika demanded.

"I'll explain it all later, Pet," Helena soothed, dismissing his demand.

"Will you let him return to the human realm alive and without further injury?" I negotiated.

"Of course, if you remain to face punishment for leading a rebellion of human sympathizers in an attempt to take the throne for yourself."

"What?" Pika asked, looking at me.

Liam looked uncomfortable with this accusation, like it was the first time he'd heard it.

"Ember...did you do this?" Pika asked.

"I agree to your terms. Will you allow me to say goodbye?" I asked Helena.

Helena curled her upper lip in disgust but nodded.

I walked to Reilley, who grimaced while shaking his head.

"Ember, no. Don't do this," he pleaded.

"I have no choice."

Reaching him, I stood on my toes to kiss him goodbye. Even hunched in defeat and pain, he was still taller than me. Tears streamed down his bruised face as our lips met tenderly.

Liam made a choking sound as he watched.

"I love you, Reilley," I whispered. Stroking his face, I added, "Don't forget to put witch hazel on those bruises." I smiled up at him and wiped his tears gently.

Suddenly, I dropped to one knee and pulled out my boot-dagger. Sliding the first jewel, I aimed it at Helena and pressed the second jewel.

The blade shot out of the hilt and stuck into the wall behind her as she stepped to the side.

"Liam, seize her," Helena ordered.

I let him pull my hands behind my back. He stood much closer than was necessary, pressing his hard cock against my back and licking my ear.

"Now, you're in trouble," he breathed in my ear.

His touch made me gag. With rage burning inside me, I was afraid I wouldn't be able to control my fire enough to burn just Helena.

"For that treason as well as conspiring to seize the throne, you will be executed," Helena proclaimed.

"No," Reilley, Pika, and Liam gasped softly.

"For treason, you say? Well, you'd know all about that," I retorted.

"Pardon me?" she said coldly.

I informed her for Pika's benefit. *I need to reach the dagger that Liam keeps at his lower back.* I leaned back against Liam as I talked, rubbing against him. His grip loosened a little, and I used my hands to caress his thighs. "How many people have you killed to get to the throne? Four? Or was it more?"

She took a step closer to me, glaring as she sniffed sharply.

That's right. Come to me.

"What?" Pika asked.

"Oh yes, didn't she tell you?"

Pika looked at Helena, and I kept distracting Liam. He breathed hard in my ear but hadn't loosened his grip any more.

"She's a traitor, my love. I've never killed anyone," Helena promised Pika.

"I guess our uncle and aunt don't count then?"

She rounded on me. "You know nothing."

"I know you killed our aunt to marry our uncle, but he wouldn't remarry so you killed him. I know you killed my mother to marry my father, and then you killed him when he was arranging my marriage to a prominent house. I know you killed Duncan because I gave him too much favor. I know you sent pirates to kidnap me and bring me here to frame me for a rebellion that doesn't exist. But there's one thing I can't figure out. Why would you send Liam to check on me to make sure I wasn't planning on returning? My guess is that he wasn't aware of your plan to frame me for treason. He only serves you because you promised *not* to kill me if he did, right? You sent him to get him out of the way for a while so he wouldn't find out that you planned to kill me after all."

Liam's grip loosened a little more as he realized the truth of my words, but he didn't let go. She was closing in on me, and I still couldn't reach around Liam to his dagger.

"I should've killed you long ago. It was foolish of me to exile you to the human realm where you could gather supporters and plot against me," she snarled.

"Are you referring to the rest of the Fae whose lives you destroyed?"

She was in my face, well within reach. *One last shot.* I reached farther up and grabbed Liam's manhood. I heard him suck in breath with a hiss of pleasure. His grip loosened, and I reached behind his back for his dagger.

"I will kill you myself. You have no idea how I've longed for this moment." Helena smiled at me with satisfaction. I had finally handed her just cause. She pulled the dagger from its decorative sheath at her waist. As I saw her raise it at me, I knew I wouldn't reach Liam's dagger in time.

I failed.

Before I felt the pierce of her blade, I heard a wet sound, a sizzle, and a painful gasp. Helena's dagger clattered to the floor as she looked down at her breast in surprise. The point of a blade grew from her heart.

As her lifeless form crumbled to the floor, Pika stood behind her. His hands were cut and bleeding from where he'd clutched my hiltless dagger. His eyes glistened with unshed tears, but he held his chin up.

"Pika." I looked at him, astonished. I rushed to embrace him and look at his wounds. They still bubbled slightly from his contact with the steel of my dagger. He let me hug and pet him, happy to be reunited.

"No!" Liam screamed as he took in Helena's corpse. He'd placed all of his hopes in one power-hungry sadist, and they'd dissolved in a pool of her blood. "How? What have you done?" Sorrow filled Liam's face: sorrow for everything he'd lost, sorrow for everything he'd given up, and sorrow for everything he'd done. With sorrow in control, he cracked and lashed out.

He pulled the dagger I'd been trying to reach and held it to Reilley's throat. "All this for one small human? Would you ever do such things for me?"

I felt the familiar rise of fire in my gut, ready to ignite my enemy. I beat it down. *Reilley's too close.* "Liam, please," I begged. The back of my throat ached at the sight of a blade at Reilley's soft neck.

"You're afraid for him? For this weak human? You'd beg for his life? You'd choose him over me? Why?"

I didn't respond, not wanting to incite him further.

"Helena is dead. Don't you see? Nothing is to stop us from finally being together. You'd like that, wouldn't you, Ember?"

I looked at Reilley. His face was calm and determined. I'd seen that expression before, and it didn't bode well.

"Well, Ember?" Liam's eyes proclaimed the lunacy that had been brewing for who knows how long.

"Yes, Liam. Whatever you want. Just let him go."

Liam smiled triumphantly and beckoned me closer. "Come, we can kill him together and put all this nonsense behind us."

I walked forward slowly. "I don't think that's necessary, Liam."

"Of course it is! Who knows what kind of mischief this meddlesome human will cook up? Besides, it would make me very happy."

I smiled my best charming smile. "Anything that will make you happy, my love."

I didn't feel bad about taking advantage of Liam's madness. He put Reilley in a chokehold and handed me the dagger to run him through.

I looked at Liam, who was high on victory. Reilley's dragon green eyes met mine with unwavering trust.

As Reilley moved his hips to the side and took a step back, his head popped out of Liam's hold. He executed the defensive move I'd taught him perfectly. Before Liam could react, his own dagger was at his throat.

"You never could beat me, Liam," I warned as I watched him try to figure out his next attack.

Defeat crumpled his face, and tears glistened in his mad, untamed eyes.

"Why?"

"You can't understand, Liam."

"But I love you."

I shook my head. "You never knew what true love was."

The torment in his eyes cleared away the madness. "That's not true, Ember. True love was why I suffered through all this."

"I'm sorry, Liam. King Pika?" I looked at my brother. "What's your verdict?"

Pika stood up straight and projected the image of a true king. "Liam, you shall be imprisoned until you have been deemed rehabilitated. Ember, keep him still while I fetch a guard."

26

When Pika returned, a guard placed manacles on Liam and another freed Reilley.

I embraced him and kissed every cut and bruise on his face. I hugged him gently, sensitive to his injuries. He wrapped his arms around me and stroked my hair. Listening to his steady heartbeat, I felt like I could breathe again. I hadn't realized I was shaking with tears until Reilley gently shushed me.

I buried my face in his chest. "I'm never leaving you again," I mumbled.

"You will never have the need," Reilley soothed.

Once my heart had started beating again, I turned to Pika.

"Brother, this is Reilley. Reilley, my brother Pika, the king of Faerie."

Reilley bowed deeply. "It's an honor to meet someone Ember holds so dear."

"Likewise."

Pika pulled Reilley away, leaving the throne

room and the pool of blood that surrounded Helena. I followed them.

"That being said, a word of caution: whatever Liam did to you will be nothing compared to what I'll do should you hurt my sister." Pika spoke with a stern voice while standing straight with his shoulders back.

I stared at Pika, speechless.

"I'd expect no less. However, excuse me for saying, you can't be as formidable as Ember herself."

"Let's not put it to the test," Pika said.

"Agreed," Reilley replied.

Pika took in Reilley's abused state, then looked down at his own bloody clothes.

"Well, I don't know about you two, but I feel like a bath and a change of clothes are in order. Ember, why don't you take Reilley to your room, and I'll send a healer and fresh garments?'

"That would be most welcome, Pika. Thank you."

I led Reilley through the palace. He wasn't so injured that the beauty was lost on him. His eyes sparkled in the golden green light like the fountains he smiled at.

It seemed my brother had insisted my room be left alone in my absence. It still showed the disarray of someone who'd packed in a hurry. The white stone walls of my bedroom were covered in places by the ivy that clung to them.

I led Reilley to my soft canopy bed, draped in curtains of shimmering green.

I helped him remove his shirt and bid him to stay.

Rather than taking him to the Fire Clan bathhouse, I grabbed a water pitcher and quickly filled it from a spring that trickled outside my bedroom door. I poured the cool water into the washbasin and used a soft cloth to gently clean his wounds.

His chest was caked with dried blood, and I blinked back tears.

Seeing my distress, he caught my hand in his and kissed my palm. "Thank you for coming for me, Ember. It's over now."

I nodded and stared into his clear, green eyes. "I'm sorry I got you into this."

"You're worth it."

A knock on the door announced the healer's arrival. He welcomed me home with a smile and went about healing Reilley's wounds. It didn't take long as they were mostly superficial. He left a change of clothes for Reilley and excused himself.

Once he'd left, I renewed the water and washed myself. I told Reilley to rest, maybe sleep a little, but his eyes followed my movements around the room.

Washed and changed, I led Reilley to a shady pool near my room. We sat watching the frogs leap from lily pad to lily pad and the fish dart around merrily.

"I knew you'd be here." Pika grinned as he approached.

We smiled up at him, and he sat and gazed at the pool for a while.

"You have much work ahead of you," I pointed out to Pika, not taking my eyes from the pool.

"I do, but won't you stay and help me?" He held

my gaze with strong eye contact in the hope that I wouldn't leave.

I smiled sadly. "I have no wish to rule or meddle any longer in the affairs of state. I want a simple life like the one I was born to."

Pika nodded his understanding. "All right, I hope that won't keep you from visiting?"

"Will human sympathizers be welcome in Faerie once more?"

"Of course. To tell you the truth, I only recently found out about the persecutions. I'm not sure Papa ever knew. She covered her tracks well, scaring any survivors so badly that they wouldn't even talk to the king. Besides, he was so trusting and kind-hearted. I don't think he could've believed it of her. I'm not sure I would've had I not seen what she did to you."

I nodded. "That would explain why they were never stopped. In any case, I will visit. Right now, I have good news to deliver to my Fae friends in the human realm."

"Where will you go after that?"

"I'm not sure. I think we'll check on Reilley's aunt."

"Well, when you're finished delivering news and checking on relatives, I'd like to give you a gift. The country home where we spent time with Papa, I want you to have it. Live there if it suits you."

I smiled at my brother's kindness. "Thank you. We will. I know you'll be a great king," I encouraged.

After a warm meal and a long sleep, we bid my brother farewell. I embraced Pika tightly and promised to meet again soon.

The reign of King Pika, King of the Purple Flame, brought joy and hope to Faerie and Fae-kind. Many Fae and half-Fae returned to Faerie to live out their long lives in peace and prosperity. Some, like myself, brought their humans with them.

EPILOGUE

As rosy dawn-light sparkled in his emerald depths, I smiled unhindered. A warmth like that of cheerful firelight on the skin filled me as I wandered the forests of his eyes. *My heart was unchained by a human with dragon green eyes and an honest heart.*

We lay in the warm bed of our country home. Reilley smiled as I snuggled deeper into the covers.

"Where are you going?" He peeked under the blankets at me.

"What do you say, Reilley? Are you up for an adventure?"

The inn tavern was dim and crowded for a sleepy country village. It seemed all the residents spent their evenings listening to the aging musician imbue the rest of his life into his guitar. Men and women alike raised their glasses and off-key voices, singing the songs they had learned long ago.

In the darkest corner, with my back to the wall, I sat as far from their rowdy merrymaking as I could. The shapely waitress, with curls that shined in the soft light, smiled as she delivered my drink. The dimples in her cheeks were becoming, and I knew I only had to give her a wink to feel her warmth that night.

"Thank you," I told her, staring into the amber liquid in the glass she'd given me.

Her plump lower lip pouted when I didn't respond to her silent offer. *She is beautiful, and I know I could help her. But not now. My mind is too full to give her the appreciation she deserves.*

"Oi, Rose!" The bartender beckoned the waitress from across the room.

She clicked her tongue before leaving to answer his call.

I blew out all my breath, then downed the drink. Running my fingertip along the smooth rim of the glass, I considered ordering another. *I should not waste what I have left. I do not know how long it will be before I get another job.* Though my position on the merchant airship had been ideal for staying on the move, I wasn't keen to fly anytime soon after what had happened with the pirates.

Closing my eyes, I could still feel the warmth of their blood as it streamed down my blade to my hand. Mac's astonishment echoed in my mind. "Sasha, where did you learn to do that?" he'd asked as I stared blankly at their lifeless forms sprawled on the deck.

Squeezing my eyes tighter, I sighed to myself. *For all my vows never to spill blood again, I did not hesitate to kill my fellow humans.* My guilt held firm even as I knew the pirates had been the worst kind of men; the world was better from them no longer in it.

And in the end, I handed Charlie over to that agent. I clenched my fist until it shook. *I followed her wishes; she said she was helping Ember.* I sighed again, relaxing my hand, and snorted to myself.

I do not know what I am so upset about. I knew Ember would never love me. I knew she would eventually find her home with Reilley. I was only involved to show them how they felt about each other. I smiled inwardly. *That is right. She could not have loved me, but I helped her still. I showed her she deserved happiness. And now she has it with Reilley, or at least I hope she does... Let it go.*

Placing money on the table, I rose from my seat and started toward the stairs and the room I'd requested for the night. *I should be able to find another job in that nearby city Mac told me of yesterday.* I took some comfort in the knowledge that he was likely back in the loving embrace of his wife and children.

I didn't bother to light the lamp as I entered the small room. I just stretched out on the bed, grateful the whiskey had relaxed me enough for sleep. Letting out a long sigh, I closed my eyes and waited for dreams to take me.

After a few even breaths, my ears pricked as a floorboard creaked ever so softly to my left. I forced myself to continue breathing slowly though my instinct was to freeze.

The strike came from above, and I was barely able to avoid it by rolling to the side. Fabric tore as a knife sank deep into the blankets beneath me.

My hand wrapped around a slender wrist in the dark while my attacker tried to reclaim the weapon.

In a fluid motion, the wrist in my grasp twisted and thin fingers clenched my wrist. I jerked my assailant's arm and pulled her off-balance onto the free spot I'd just occupied before she got a chance to yank the blade out with her other hand. Twisting my hips, I wrapped my legs around her neck, putting her in a choke hold.

Her arms flailed at my hips to no avail as I squeezed my thighs.

"Who sent you?" I asked the assassin in my mother tongue.

She growled in frustration but did not answer.

"Was it the Ubyzniki? My father? Who?"

"Go to Hell," she spat in Russian.

I clenched my teeth and tightened my hold until she went limp with unconsciousness. Sighing heavily, I allowed my tense muscles to relax.

After a few more deep breaths, I slipped off the bed and fumbled for a match on the side table. The warm, flickering light of the lamp illuminated the room and the crumbled assassin in my bed.

Her long, dark hair had begun to loosen from her braid and fell partially over her face. I reached out and gently brushed the soft tresses aside. Her skin had a warm undertone, and a smattering of freckles dusted her cheeks. I held my finger above her full lips and was relieved to feel the telltale signs of life.

Tilting my head, I regarded her. *I have never seen her before. I thought I knew everyone in the Ubyzniki.* I pursed my lips. *Then again, I have not seen them for many years. She could have joined since then. On the other hand, she looks only a few years younger than I. The Ubyzniki train their members young, and they do not let just anyone in. Perhaps it is not them after all.*

I shook my head and pulled my surprisingly light attacker until she lay her on her stomach. After rummaging through the pack I'd salvaged from the pirate shipwreck, I found the rope and used it to tie her hands and feet.

Her knife, which I retrieved from the bed, was a

nicely balanced stiletto. I admired the craftsmanship, running my thumb gently along the sharp edge.

"Very nice," I told her.

But she was still unconscious.

I crossed the room to the washbasin I'd used earlier that evening.

After a satisfying splash, the assassin gasped awake.

"Let us talk," I said when she was done sputtering.

AFTERWORD

Thank you for reading! I do so hope you enjoyed it. If you have a moment, I would very much appreciate a review on the store where you bought it. Tell other readers what you thought, and help them make a decision on this book.

If you'd like to stay updated on news about my books and events, you can subscribe to my newsletter on my website: www.dlieber.com

On my site, you will also find my blog, where I post all my fun little tidbits.

Thanks again! I hope you will travel through my worlds with me again in the future.

D. Lieber

ABOUT THE AUTHOR

D. Lieber has a wanderlust that would make a butterfly envious. When she isn't planning her next physical adventure, she's recklessly jumping from one fictional world to another. Her love of reading led her to earn a Bachelor's in English from Wright State University.

Beyond her skeptic and slightly pessimistic mind, Lieber wants to believe. She has been many places—from Canada to England, France to Italy, Germany to Russia—believing that a better world comes from putting a face on "other." She is a romantic idealist at heart, always fighting to keep her feet on the ground and her head in the clouds.

Lieber lives in Wisconsin with her husband (John) and cats (Yin and Nox).

LINKS

Website: www.dlieber.com
Goodreads: www.goodreads.com/dlieber writing
Bookbub: www.bookbub.com/profile/d-lieber